S.J. WIST

SHATTERED
GUARDIANS

Infinity Dreamt Books

Published by Infinity Dreamt

Author's website: www.sjwist.com

ISBN: 978-0-9916914-2-5

1

LATE THAT EVENING, Tori wasn't sure if she had meditated herself into the Walkway or not as nothing looked the same. The different dimension of her city was usually a dark world, with buildings acting as antennas of the dark energy that rose from the streets below. The Walkway was the world of nightmares, where demons and spirits were very real. These spirits were known to the physical world as Whispers, and they made themselves seen by possessing stone statues. Their counterparts, Wraiths, could tear down the walls of any building they wanted, and usually made themselves seen by the destruction they caused.

It had been Wraiths controlled by the Diruo that had killed her mother when they had brought down Tori's whole building. The only light that existed in the Walkway were the small, glowing spheres of people's souls. There lived thousands of people in her city, but she never saw more than a few dozen souls at a time. It was as if whatever had given her power over the Whispers and her ability to enter the Walkway as a Hush, also had the ability to limit her foresight.

It was hard for Tori to see the difference between the present and the future while she stood before a graveyard.

Death never answered to anyone, it simply was and would always be, regardless of what she did now, had done in the past, or what she would strive to salvage with what was to come. Ultimately everyone she cared about would die one way or another.

'You are beginning to understand the futility of your defiance.'

Tori turned her light blue eyes to the end of the graveyard where a particular tombstone caught her attention, while the eerily familiar voice drifted away from her mind. She didn't remember that particular grave being there when she visited this place the last time. It was a visit that had ended with a vicious battle with the Wraith inhabitant that guarded the graveyard; the same Wraith who seemed content to haunt her thoughts now.

Tori looked around for the dark stone angel, and contemplated going over the old iron fence that separated where she was standing now on the sidewalk from the grounds of death. Her gargoyle hadn't come with her, and if the angel Wraith did decide to attack her again, Pug had already proven that he was next to helpless to protect her from it. When she looked back at the tombstone, the choice looked to have already been made for her; for the gargoyle's wings that sheltered the gravestone was not something she could ignore. Not when it looked so much like her own Pug.

She put her foot up in the space between the spokes of the fence and then jumped over, landing on a flower bed that looked to be long forgotten. It lay twisted with dying vines and broken and misplaced pieces of garbage and other things of her world. It all looked to have been disintegrating for over a hundred years.

Tori focused back on what she was here for and started walking carefully between the graves for her target. When she reached it, she looked for just whose name was inscribed on the grave, but it was blank. Tori looked up into the lifeless eyes of the gargoyle over it that was as tall as her. It too seemed to lack any clues to just what the purpose of it being here was.

"Do you like it?"

The voice hit Tori's spine like a cold knife in the back, and she turned around to find herself face to face with the angel Wraith. It still hid its face under a living stone hood that could pass it as some hermit or wise old man. Only Tori knew better, and it didn't take a long sword that it held in its human-like carved hands to tell her that.

"I asked you a question."

"I don't answer to you," Tori replied as her best survival instinct kicked in when scared; the one to fight.

"Why do you insist on fighting when you cannot hope to win? You can see the ultimate futility of your resistance. It's what brought you here. It is your fate to die, along with the rest of your kind."

"Apparently not, because I don't see a name on this grave, demon," Tori spat back. "Besides, when the world is covered in darkness, who will you have left to torment?"

"Despite what you might think, I take no pleasure in your suffering. Only death brings me comfort and more voices to keep me company. The screams of the living are aggravating to say the least."

"You should try living sometime, you

might like it more," Tori mocked in reply.

The angel laughed and walked closer to the unmarked grave, trailing its long, living stone cloak behind it. "You already know that all Whispers, Wraiths, and gargoyles were alive once. I am one of the oldest, but I am not the first."

"Is that what you're after? Power?" Tori asked, wanting to pry as much information that she could during her risky visit here.

"I don't want power. I just want a finality to it all. My existence, if one could call it such, is a limbo that constantly sways from the living to the dead, and back to the living. It becomes exhausting after thousands of years. To change it, one must possess the Hush who is heard by all of our kind."

"And who's that?" Tori asked.

"You already know who it is, but you

refuse to accept the truth that has been laid down before your own eyes. No matter. Does a grave guarded by a gargoyle truly need a name? What would you like? Hero? Martyr? Lost cause?"

Tori refused to let the Wraith unnerve her. "It must drive something like you crazy to not be able to see what you alone have self-entitled yourself to see. Hope must be one hell of a pain in the side. Even if it is just blind hope that we have." She started to leave then, but the dark angel stopped her in her tracks with its sword outstretched in her path. "Let me pass."

"Hope can die with the one carrying it."

"Hope doesn't die, you should know that. If you kill me, you will only make your circumstances worse. The hope that we will survive has already spread around the world, and it can't be stopped."

"You hide behind others and their blind faith in you far too much. No, I think I will inscribe your grave with COWARD. You are no vessel for love or hope. The only reason you have been allowed to live this long is solely to give the illusion of such. That dream will drive you straight to your ultimate fate."

Tori backed away from the angel as its eyes began to glow red and its softened, gray stone body began to seemingly turn black as if being singed by an invisible fire. "I'm not scared of you or any of your kind."

"You should be. We were here long before your kind became the instruments that entertain us. We will be here long after humankind is a mere memory. Your regret will not allow you to escape us. We have already won this war. Now it's just a matter of watching what's left, burn." The blackened angel then exploded into flames and sent them straight to her.

Tori woke with a start and cried out when someone caught her with their strong arms. The world spun madly, but she recognized the touch and cinnamon scent of the one who was holding her. "Cae."

"Hey, easy. You have to be more careful to not wander away from your body in the Walkway when you're asleep."

The room stopped burning, and she could see now that it was her room. Her nightmares were real, and she had been there for them. Everything the Wraith had said was for real, and if it wanted to, it could likely have snuffed out her soul right there and then. Pug had done nothing to get between them, and it only deepened her fears even more that she might never get the gargoyle she once knew back again. She looked at Cae, and he waited for her to say something in return. "What are you doing in here?"

"You cried out just before you woke up. You likely woke up half of the floor. If it makes you feel better, I brought a chaperone." He pointed then at her bedroom door where a hand giving the thumbs up appeared, before slipping back out and closing the door.

"Matthew heard me too?" Tori asked, growing increasingly embarrassed.

"We're taking turns in keeping an eye on you. What did you see in the Walkway?"

Tori looked away from Cae and to her blanket. "It was nothing new." She was lying to his face, and she wasn't sure why.

"What do you need?" Cae asked, wanting nothing more than to help her.

She could see his concern for her in his brown eyes, and she was to blame for it, as all she did was always push him away. The last thing she was feeling like at the moment was girlfriend material, and all he wanted of her was to look away from her war path long enough to see him. "Can you take me to the graveyard tomorrow?"

"The one with that crazy stone angel that smashed Pug and nearly killed us? Why would you want to go there?" Cae asked, perplexed.

"Can you, please?" Tori pleaded, knowing that if the dark Wraith was setting a trap, she didn't want to be taking it on alone.

"Alright, but we're bringing the whole crew with us this time."

Tori nodded and watched as he got up off of her bed. Their whole 'crew' wasn't as large of a group as he made it sound. The

Hush, Jade, from the destroyed Institute in Japan and her nephew, Kenji, were reliable and trustworthy allies. Matthew was still a kid but dependable and born a genius. Cae was likely the strongest amongst them, but Tori knew that if the horrible choice ever came to them between saving humanity and saving the ones they cared about, humanity would be toast.

"I'm just next door if you need anything else, unless you're okay with me staying in here?" Cae asked, distracting her from her chilling thoughts.

"I'll be alright."

He nodded and then left her room, leaving the door slightly open.

Tori looked around her room, before noticing that Pug was sitting just outside her window. He was as silent and still as a statue, with his wings covering most of his crouched body. She tried to reach out with her thoughts to him, but he remained unresponsive. The dark angel had done this to him, and she wanted some kind of answer on how to cure him. She promised him that she would do everything she could tomorrow to bring the gargoyle she once knew back to her. She needed an ally on the same page as her; even if she wasn't sure that she could choose the world over the ones she loved, herself. It was a sad realization, as she had likely been selected to begin with as friendship and love were not something that had been important to her before. Tori feared that the angel may have been right; they had already lost, and it was because of her.

2

THE FOLLOWING DAY, Cae drove Tori, Matthew and Kenji to the graveyard. After everything that had happened here the last time, she knew that she was taking a big risk, for they might get attacked again.

"So what are we looking for, Boss?" Matthew asked and tucked his hands into his gray coat's pocket to warm them from the cold, late winter winds.

"Names. I need the names on every

single headstone in this graveyard," Tori replied.

"Is there someone in particular who we are looking for?" Cae asked from where he stood next to her.

"Yes. Someone with my last name. Or related in some way to the Hush. I don't know. All I know is that there is someone buried here who the Wraith angel didn't want me to see."

"Speaking of devils," Cae added and nodded in the direction of where the Wraith angel continued to act oblivious to their presence, "should we take him out now? Pug and my lion should be enough to handle him this round."

"Hey, I can help too," Matthew said and pulled out his Whisper sparrow from his pocket.

Tori wiped her runny nose with the back of her glove as she contemplated how a little sparrow would be able to do anything at all in a hardcore fight.

"Give her a minute, she's gonna upgrade herself," Matthew said, and threw Feather up into the air where she promptly flew away.

Cae looked back at the Wraith angel that had stopped its rounds to stand and stare at them from under its stone-cloth hood. "If we're going to do this, we need to move before he has a chance to call any friends."

As if hearing him, the angel began to walk towards them, and pulled out its long sword from under its cloak.

"You know, I somehow get the feeling he has no friends...or any living enemies for that matter." Matthew panicked.

Pug landed between them and the angel in the entrance of the graveyard, and the Wraith stopped walking.

Tori tried to reach her thoughts out to Pug to get him to give her some idea of just what was going on, but he wouldn't answer her. So she closed her eyes and looked into the Walkway, and saw the angel Wraith's skeletal form and Pug in the life-like state that the Walkway gave to him. Still, she couldn't hear anything. Their showdown was a silent one, and it made her worry even more. When she opened her eyes, Cae caught her arm in concern.

"What's going on?"

"I don't know. I can't hear anything."

"Are they arguing in the Walkway or something?"

Tori looked around as she could now hear other voices, and just like Cae had predicted, several once-statues were now walking towards them. They weren't as alone in this fight as they thought. Several

Whispers in animal statues of all kind were backing them up.

"This is gonna get crazy at any moment. We should get out of here," Cae said.

"No--Pug is doing this because he wants me to get into this graveyard. We have to hurry before this Mexican showdown starts shooting." Tori didn't wait for Cae to reply, and ran into the cemetery. She stopped a meter from the Wraith angel, but it kept its gaze on Pug. Immediately she, Cae, and Matthew split up and started to scan the names on the tombstones. Many of them had been covered with dirt and foliage, and it slowed them down even more.

"Here!" Matthew called to them. Tori and Cae trotted over to him, and all of them looked at the tombstone marked 'Yvon Calas' on it.

"My sister's grave?" Tori said in disbelief.

"Okay, now what?" Cae said, growing increasingly uneasy with the standoff between the Wraiths and Whispers set to happen at any moment, with them in the center of it all.

"I don't know. I didn't think this far ahead," Tori replied.

They all looked back then when Pug walked over to them, and his giant self towered over them for an unobstructed view of the tombstone. Then without warning, he lifted his claws and struck the earth covering the grave.

"What the hell is he doing?" Cae asked as he took Tori's arm to pull her out of the way, but she was equally as shocked as him.

"Pug, stop it!" Tori yelled at him, but he didn't listen. She tried to grab the gargoyle's arm, but he shoved her aside. "Leave my sister's grave alone!"

Pug didn't stop, and Cae caught Tori's arm to pull her away from the sight of her sister's long-decomposed body that could only happen next. Tori didn't look away, nor could she as Pug grabbed the wooden lid of the coffin and ripped it off.

Matthew braved the sight first and peered in. "What the...? It's empty."

"What?" Cae and Tori said at the same time and dared to look inside next.

Cae looked back as he heard something move, and it was just in time to see that the patience from the Wraith angel had run out as it was lifting its sword to strike them down. "Yep. Time's up! Let's go!"

Tori didn't get a chance to argue when Pug grabbed her with claws that were still covered in the earth that had covered

Yvon's grave, and took to the air.

She looked back down, fearful for Matthew and Cae, but they got lost in the clash of Wraiths and Whispers. The living statues quickly turned the graveyard into a clouded war zone of dust and shattering stone.

3

"I SURE HOPE you found what you were looking for," Cae said as he shook his leather jacket out and threw it over a chair in his room back at the Institute.

"She just watched her sister's grave get dug up, you inconsiderate ass," Matthew snapped at Cae as he entered the room last behind them.

"By her own gargoyle, in case you missed that part," Cae added bitterly.

"My sister is still alive," Tori said from where she sat trembling on Cae's bed, and it was enough to halt their bickering for now.

"That's impossible," Cae said, his brown eyes furrowing. "An empty grave doesn't mean she's alive, Tori. Anyone could have taken her body, or maybe she was cremated."

"Have you thought about what this could mean? If my sister is alive--I mean, what if there was a way to come back to life after going dead for some time because you're in the Walkway? We're talking like beyond what the Whispers and gargoyles can do--it would be like immortality."

Cae sighed and sat down on his bed, and dropped his gaze to the blue carpet. "There are any number of people who might have stolen her body to make you think that. They want to send you searching further from here in the Walkway where they can trap you. They broke whatever and whoever Pug's essence was. They wouldn't have done that if they didn't have the intention to go for you next."

"And what if you're wrong?" Tori asked, crossing her arms in front of her.

"Tori, please, stop. We lost countless Whispers out there today along with any chance of making the normal world believe we're not the ones who are set out to destroy it."

"Do you think that the Silence gives a damn how many people it inconveniences in its conquest? Why don't you see that we can't just sit here and wait for the end of the world to knock on the Institutes door?"

"They won't need to come to our door

if you get yourself killed!" Cae shouted at her. "If you die, then all of this is over! You're the only Hush left alive who can do anything about the Silence!"

Tori whipped her gaze away from him, and then stamped out of his room. "I'm not the only one, but if anything I'm certainly the worst choice."

"Tori, that's not true and you know that," Matthew called after her.

She pretended to not hear him. Deep down inside she knew she was right back to square one: on her own. Tori didn't stop walking until she reached her room and immediately slammed the door behind her. Pug sat outside her room on her balcony. His claws were still covered in caked-on dirt, and when he turned to look at her, she walked closer and started yelling at him, "Why the hell did you do that? Do you know something about my sister?"

Pug replied with silence but stood up on his hind feet and reached out his gray, clawed hands to pick her up. Tori considered just how much trust she had left in the gargoyle and let him lift her up. Then with one harsh downbeat from his wings, they were in the air. As they continued to climb, Tori wondered where they were going. Her trust was falling to pieces with Pug, but she knew she didn't have a choice. He had risked himself and there was no saying how many Whispers had died defending them at the graveyard, so she could only assume that it was important.

Pug started flying in a different direction, and Tori looked down to where they hovered over a small, old church. He set them down near the front entrance, and Tori gave a precautionary look around.

Once upon a time it might have been a beautiful place. Now, the church that Tori stood before looked as if it had seen, felt, and survived the Apocalypse, only to come back in time to stand before her now. It may as well have for Tori had no good memories of this place. This place was the reason she had lost her best friend so many years ago, and what made the memory even more painful was that it had been her fault.

Images of Mary standing before her door beaten and bleeding still haunted her memories, and she closed her eyes to try and shut them out of her head. Tori had made a mistake. All she had to do was walk away from the gang that taunted them and none of it would have happened. They would have left them alone and she would still have her best friend, and more importantly, Mary would never have been hurt so badly.

The more she tried to convince herself that it wasn't her fault, the more she realized that some things never changed in people. Tori had yet to learn how to admit defeat and walk away. But none of her past made sense to just why she had been brought here now.

4

WHEN PUG RETURNED her to the Institute in the darkness of morning, Tori regretted all the times that she had scorned the appearance of the school as it was before her fight with Kali. Now it looked more like a high-security prison than a place to learn. There was little left of anything of a typical school now as barbed wire-topped fences surrounded the Institute, and stumps replaced the once-beautiful tree-lined grounds. Trees gave something to hide behind and the fence was to keep out the unwanted visitors. Spies and on more than one occasion, the homeless and desperate sought the school to hide where their powers wouldn't get them imprisoned. What the Institute truly existed for was public now, but for some reason the police hadn't chased them all out into the streets just yet.

She felt like a traitor who didn't deserve to be here. Her responsibility was to the school now, not chasing her own family issues all over the city. The idea of her older sister being alive sent a surge of hope through Tori's veins. Would Yvon have aged? Would she still be as young as the day she supposedly died? Would Yvon be the reason that their father was content to ignore the supposed last Hush in the world?

A million questions and less than a handful of answers sent Tori's eyes drifting to the other side of the fence. A reporter and her van stood outside, giving some kind of live and on the scene report. With her luck, she would be on the morning news on TV. Again.

"They still won't go away," Cae's voice said from behind her.

"Anyone talk to them yet?" Tori asked as she turned around to face Cae. He didn't seem to know about her little fly-out yet, and she was content to keep it that way, as much as she hated continually lying to him.

"Just what should we say? 'Congratulations on finding the only Whisper school in the country and helping to make it into a prison? And that this school of kids is not trying to kill everyone?' It wouldn't matter, because they already have their own story of just what is going on. I'm just glad they haven't set up posts for a witch-burning event yet."

She sighed and changed her focus to apologizing for their fight earlier. He didn't seem upset, and she found that she was no longer angry, either.

"I'm sorry for yelling at you earlier," Cae started.

"It's alright. I get it. I'm here to save the world, and any kind of personal stake I have in it doesn't have any place in that objective."

"That's not what I meant earlier. It's just that we have our hands full, and if we can deal with the problems in front of us first, then I'm all up for dealing with impossible ones later."

There was no escaping the fact that

Cae was different now and he had even taken to a more of a war-like appearance by shaving his soft brown hair off entirely despite her protests. Tori lowered her head with his added weight to the subject. He was just as stressed out as she was, and it showed in his brown eyes. "I'm worried, Cae."

"Did you see something?"

"If the media has us as the enemy now, then I don't know what we can do. I fear that the government is going to move against us soon."

"What do you want to do?"

Tori didn't know how he would take to her idea. She still didn't know how she was taking to it. "We don't stand a chance against trained combat professionals, even with the help of the Whispers. The Whispers won't fatally injure them unless I command them to, and our enemies know this by now. We have to recruit something that can take them on without my head having to be everywhere at once."

"We don't have the kind of money needed to hire mercenaries, if that's what you were thinking," Cae replied. "And I really don't like the idea of looking for Wraith handlers."

"Neither do I." Tori let out a long sigh as her thoughts ended with no answers. "Maybe we'll get lucky and some kind of an opportunity will present itself. Surely the media would have sparked the attention of something more than what this city has to offer?"

"Maybe," Cae replied.

"What are you thinking?"

Cae let out a long sigh, letting whatever he was thinking leave him. "It's nothing. Let's just do our rounds and try and get some sleep for now." He headed into the school and Tori gave one last look at the perimeter fence before following after him.

She had promised his father, Headmaster Deron, to help keep the peace and students in order at night where needs be, and it was a welcome distraction from what the outside of her school looked like. This was the only home she had now, and Tori would do everything in her power to protect it. Even if it was now the center of an incoming war.

5

TORI COULDN'T FOCUS on anything the next morning in gym class and the beating that Cae was giving Matthew in combat training wasn't helping. Everyone around her was changing and adapting to the harsher circumstances they had to endure now. Even Cae had become colder and more determined, and sooner or later the barrier that kept him from losing it on her would fade and she would see his real self that he kept hidden. If there was another side to see in him like there had been with his brother, Vincent.

She dropped her head to her hands and tried to not think about Vincent. About his warning. About his threat to do everything in his power to control her and win this war. The whole world was at war with them. She forced her mind to ignore all of Vincent's shows of affection and reminded herself that he was the enemy now. A cunning enemy that would stoop as low as to say he cared about her while readying a knife to stab her in the back.

"Tori. Tori!"

Tori looked up at Matthew, who stared down at her impatiently, before looking at Cae next to him who looked to be equally concerned. "What?"

"Hate to interrupt your daydreaming, but you're up," Matthew said.

"I already told you that I won't fight you--not even in training. It goes against my morals." She glowered at Cae when he laughed.

"And it goes against my morals to beat up my girlfriend, so you don't have a choice," Cae added.

"Sure I do," Tori replied. "Where's Kenji?"

"He up and vanished like the ninja he is. Again," Matthew replied.

"Well, I didn't really feel like practicing today. I'll be up in my room." She had only made it a few steps before Cae ran over to her and caught her in a tight bear hug from behind. She tried to playfully break free, but when she had enough, so did her reflexes. Tori vanished from his grip and into the Walkway, leaving him and Matthew scratching their heads and shrugging their shoulders in defeat. Careful not to touch or displace either of their bright souls, she carefully made her way out of the gym, before stopping at the door when Cae's lion pushed it open and stuck its head in. In the Walkway, its hair and flesh looked alive and not a leathery living stone. It looked right at her. "Shoo!" she said, wanting it to get out of the way. It didn't obey her and instead sat down.

Tori tried the more forceful approach against the giant Whisper that was still taller than her when sitting, and attempted to squeeze her way past it. Only that was met with an angry growl and flare of teeth. It was enough to break her concentration and snap her right back into her world.

"Hah, now I got you!" Cae said triumphantly as he pounced on her again and caught her upper arm.

Tori remained frozen in place and staring at his Whisper. "Did you see what your lion did just now?"

"Huh?" Cae asked and let go of her arm before looking at his Whisper. "It turned to stone shortly after coming in here."

"It growled and flared its teeth at me in the Walkway--and it wouldn't move."

"They can't do that--not to you. You sure you're not--?"

"Dammit, for the last time I'm not seeing things!" she snapped furiously at him and then focused back on the door. Pug was already nearby when Cae's lion opened its eyes as the larger gargoyle grabbed it by the back of its neck and pulled it out of the doorway and into the hallway. The lion twisted and nearly struck Pug with an angry swipe of claws before taking off down the hall like a crazed cat fleeing a bathtub.

"That was...unusual," Matthew said out loud.

"Yeah," Cae added.

Tori was just as lost as to what was going on with Cae's Whisper, and left at that.

6

WHEN IT CAME to warfare, Tori figured that starting where the Institute's potential army was stashed couldn't hurt. It was just as dark as she remembered when she made her way into the basement with the largest flashlight she could find. As she reached the last steps, several torches on the walls suddenly lit up and illuminated the room.

"I was wondering when you would

return."

Tori was just about to click off her flashlight before the appearance of a familiar voice, but instead beamed it at the giant snake that sat upright on the last step before her. "What are you doing back here?"

"Well, you did leave the door open. Perhaps I was also rather presumptuous at the time," the snake answered.

"I want you to leave," Tori replied.

"If you insist," the snake said as it lowered its torso to the ground, "but before I go, I was curious to whether you had found the 'God in the Machine' yet?"

Tori's chin lifted higher as the snake presented an interesting problem. She had assumed that the monster of a machine that Kali had been hooked up to in the Arc was what had been this 'Machine,' but now the snake suggested otherwise.

"Ah, so you haven't. Tick tock, Tori, humanity's survival is on the clock." The snake started to slither away at that.

"Wait!" Tori called after it.

The snake stopped but didn't look back at her.

"You know where it is, don't you?" Tori asked.

"Perhaps. But my information is not free."

"What do you want?" Tori asked more out of curiosity than with any intention of giving this snake Wraith anything. It was then that her eye caught sight of Kenji's samurai Whisper not far behind the snake, pretending to be one of the other lifeless stone statues that lined the room. It slightly lowered its face and Tori could sense its thoughts. If this snake decided to get mean, she could easily have the

Whisper cut it to pieces with its katana.

"For you to destroy it on finding it of course."

"Freeing you and all the Wraiths from its control? Of course, I should have seen it before. You're enslaved too, aren't you little snake?"

The snake returned an angry hiss at her.

"So who's your master?"

"You will meet her soon enough, but for now, I will give you--" The snake's words were cut from it suddenly when Kenji's samurai came to life. In two quick steps forward, it brought its katana down on the neck of the snake, separating its head from its body. Then it crumbled into black stone dust.

It had all happened so fast that when Tori's mind had finally caught up to what the samurai had just done, it was already aiming its blade to the armor on its own stomach. She forced her will on the Whisper to stop, but if it did hear her, it didn't obey as it drove the blade through itself and joined the stone dust of the snake as dust itself.

Tori backed away, only to fall against the stairs behind her. Then one after the other, the torches in the room extinguished themselves and left her in complete darkness.

***

Tori didn't know how long she had been out for before the scent of cinnamon rolls woke her up. Matthew had pushed an entire plate of them before her nose. She stared at them for a while, not moving from where she rested her head on her arms on the cafeteria table. Then she shot up straight on remembering what had happened in the basement of the Institute. On looking at the clock, she saw that it was almost the end of lunch hour.

"I was beginning to think that you had fallen into a coma," Matthew said.

Tori blinked as her mind raced to catch up to the present time. "How did I get here?"

"I found you passed out on the basement stairs. When I asked you if you were okay, you said yes and got up, walked here and passed out on this cafeteria table."

Tori didn't have any memory of walking herself here, but the last thing she wanted to do was give Matthew another worry that she might be going crazy for real. His concerned face suggested that he might be already thinking just that.

"You've been sleeping a lot lately.

What are you and Cae doing all night?"

Tori's face went beet-red from how he had suggested that they were doing something other than working, and she quickly stuffed away all following thoughts with a cinnamon roll. Matthew seemed so much older today, and she could see that the kid was growing up at an alarming rate. It had been almost a year since she came to the Institute, but he looked like he had put on five more since their first meeting after Pug had kidnaped and brought her here for the first time. His freckles were starting to fade and he was taking more care to his red hair that he wore styled neatly to the side. He looked less like a child now and more like a man. Or had she just been asleep that long?

"Tori?" Matthew asked with growing worry.

"I'm okay," she assured him after swallowing the last of the cinnamon roll. "I've just been more busy than usual."

"Well, I don't want to give you even more work, but when did you want to start looking for clues to where your father is?"

"I already started. If we find Vincent or Kali, we will find my father."

"Bloody hell, the Diruo's Hush is still alive?"

"I think so," Tori replied.

"And Vincent won't be easy to find. Well, I can tell you for sure that it's not the Arc--there isn't enough left of that place to scrap together for a toaster."

"Yeah," Tori replied. "Question is if they're not working for the government, then just what are their intentions?"

"So you want to stage a family reunion to find out? That's rather deceitful of you to think up," Matthew said with a grin on his face.

"I'd rather have a sickening family reunion then get the surprise deal of a mess of whatever they're conjuring up."

"Well, we can't go in blind," Matthew said as his eyes drifted to the table as he fell into deeper thought on the topic.

"What do you suggest?" Tori asked with interest.

"I figured we could start at Whispering Stone. That was the where your father and Headmaster Deron used to work before here, right?"

"Isn't it still like under government control?" Tori asked.

"When has that ever stopped us?" Matthew said with a wider mischievous grin that brought back a childish face that Tori more easily recognized. "But if you really want the thrill of breaking into a government facility ruined, it has been abandoned for a while."

"Abandoned? Are you sure?"

Matthew just shrugged in reply. "I've had Feather watch it for days, and we didn't see anyone come in or out."

"Fine, but you're telling Cae. He's about to lock me into a birdcage for my own safety at this point."

Matthew laughed. "Darn, you weren't supposed to know about that cage until your birthday." He ducked as he got up to leave as Tori returned a scornful look.

She looked at the clock in the cafeteria again after Matthew had left as time felt like it was going by faster today. Figuring she was just overtired, she took a couple more cinnamon rolls with her before leaving to find Kenji. If they were going to head to the old Whispering Stone Institute, she needed to cross off the possibility of being crazy beforehand.

7

TORI STRETCHED OUT her thoughts in search of Kenji's Samurai Whisper. She found them both in his room, where Kenji looked to be fencing with his Whisper. He had cut his black hair shorter, and wore a dark blue kimono as if he were attending a special event. Tori continued to watch them for a while before Kenji took notice of her presence and the both of them stopped.

"Hey, Tori."

"Kenji," Tori said, starting right at the point of her visit, "has your samurai been missing at all lately?"

"Missing?" Kenji asked, and then looked at his Whisper. "No, he's been with me most of the time. I use him to watch over Jade when I sleep as well. Is something wrong?"

"No, no," Tori replied hastily. "I just had a nightmare, and now I'm completely certain it was just because of our attack on the Arc that it was triggered."

"How many nightmares have you been having lately? Jade has had some unusual ones as well--ones that look and feel like real life or the Walkway but they aren't."

"What has she seen?" Tori asked curiously.

"I can badger her for hours, but she won't tell me," Kenji said as he set his blade on the rack on the wall.

"Well, tell her to stay strong. Kali is alive and likely twice as angry as before. She could be trying to mess with our heads."

"What have you seen in these nightmares?" Kenji asked with concern.

Tori thought about how to tell him without causing too much of an uproar. "Last one I saw your samurai Whisper act on its own to silence a Wraith."

"That's what they are designed to do-- fight the Wraiths," Kenji added.

"I know. But this Wraith--" Tori stopped there, as it would have likely been heard wrong by him. "Never mind. If it was just a nightmare, then it was just that."

"Be careful, Tori. Wraiths are demons of lies and deceit. It wouldn't tell you anything that would not benefit itself tenfold and put you in serious danger."

Tori nodded, knowing that already, even if she was testing the boundaries of it a little too far as of late. First the graveyard, then the nightmare. Whatever the Diruo's plans were, it included pushing her over the line of good and evil. "I know."

"Well, if you need any help, we're here," Kenji offered.

"I'm going to need your help soon. Matthew is working on a plan for visiting the old Whispering Stone Institute. Hopefully, it's a quiet one, but I'm all for having a sword or two nearby."

"We'll be ready," Kenji said reassuringly and his Whisper sheathed its blade.

Tori turned around and left the room, feeling weirder by the second. If she didn't get a grip, the Diruo would walk all over them without her seeing a thing.

8

IT TOOK TORI a good three minutes to get Headmaster Deron's attention that afternoon as he seemed to be daydreaming while staring at the wall of his office. When he did come around, his face looked as if she had shaken him out of a nightmare. "Headmaster?"

"Oh, Tori," he said as he pulled a handkerchief from his pocket and wiped his forehead. "I didn't see you there."

"Are you alright? It looked as if you were having a waking nightmare."

"I'm all right," he replied and adjusted himself in his desk chair. "I was just practicing something with my Whisper from what Cae had shown me. I have to figure out how to look at my Great Dane's mind and see what he's seeing without leaving my body so vulnerable in the process."

Tori briefly looked around the room, before looking to the door of his office as his dog Whisper pushed it further open and came in. The large dog walked over to the Headmaster's desk then and sat down before turning into solid stone. "You can see through his eyes?"

"A little. Cae is a lot better at it than I am," the Headmaster said and adjusted his chair to better face her. "So what can I help you with, Tori?"

Tori was now thinking about all the times Cae's lion Whisper had stalked her and how he had even seen her through Pug's eyes when his question came about. Did his lion growling at her in the Walkway have anything to do with his ability? "I, uh," she said and quickly brought her mind back to the present. "I was just wondering, did you have any enemies when you worked at the Whispering Stone Institute?"

"Hmm, I don't think so. There weren't a whole lot of us on the project at the time. There weren't a whole lot of people who knew about the Whispers at all. We were nothing more than a group of real-life Ghostbusters from what I can imagine."

"That must have been interesting to bring up at the cocktail parties."

Deron laughed and then leaned back

in his chair. "Well, at least our circles believe us now."

Tori only gave a small smile in return. How he had said 'our' when her mother was dead and her father was head of the Diruo unnerved her.

If the Headmaster saw any change in the look on her face, he failed to show it on his own. "Have you seen anything new?" he asked as he rested his arms on his desk.

"I've just been having some weird nightmares lately. It's almost like they're messages scrambled in death threats."

"Your mother saw a lot of crazy things, but Philip and I realized early on that she was anything but crazy. You inherited her gift just like Cae inherited mine. Perhaps you simply need to change your perspective of what you've seen so that you can see what the real messages are."

"That still doesn't narrow down the enemy numbers very much," Tori replied.

"Lots of things have changed as of late. The project I started at Whispering Stone with your parents isn't just a quiet little lab anymore--it's taken on a worldwide scale. Even if we manage to defeat the Diruo, we will always have enemies. Perhaps when the threat is over, the Whispers will disappear again and things will return to normal, but it may be a day very far away to say the least."

"I suppose you're right. Guess my dreams of being a normal teenage girl aren't going to happen anytime soon."

"Being normal is overrated. You're an extraordinary young woman, and I know, even without Melissa's foresight on the matter when she was alive, that you are destined for great things."

Tori smiled. "Thanks, Headmaster. I

really needed to hear that."

Deron gave her a nod of approval and she turned to leave his office at that, with a bit of confidence stacked back on her shoulder and even more uncertainty.

9

TORI FOUND HERSELF on her own again in her search for answers. Suspecting everyone around her would get her nowhere, and there weren't a lot of opportunities for her to just be left alone to think. She refused to be fearful of the Walkway and the visions it gave her, for they might be the only things capable of keeping everyone safe. She needed to keep herself from doing anything in them that might be dangerous in the real world--like killing someone.

She gave a momentary look at Pug, who was sitting beside her in the Hush chamber, and then closed her eyes so she could re-open them in the Walkway. The general scenery was the expected dark and gloomy, but there wasn't any of the Silence's dark energy emanating from the walls around her. At least it hadn't reached here yet.

She headed to the rooftop, as the brightly-lit souls flickered around her, oblivious to her presence. The Whispers belonging to the handlers in the school did see her as clear as day but gave her little mind. The Walkway was the best way to sneak out of the school without anyone raising the alarm of her absence. Pug picked her up and took to the air, flying her away from the Institute. But instead of heading to where Matthew said the old Whispering Stone Institute was, she had her gargoyle land them before the same church she had visited before.

Tori emerged from the Walkway and looked around, unsure of just what she was doing. Had something in her finally struck a chord of terror to send her searching for the worst person for help? Or was she really losing her nerve? She stood in silence for a while, contemplating what to do next. Vincent wasn't here, nor did she expect him to be. "Is Vincent here?" she asked Pug.

The gargoyle closed its yellow glowing eyes for a moment, before opening them and shaking his head.

"Is that the start of you speaking to me again?" Tori asked Pug.

The gargoyle looked at her and blinked slowly, before looking at the church.

Without a word, he reached out his hand to grab her, but before he could, something struck him from behind and diverted his attention.

Tori looked too as several men opened fire on them, and quickly took cover behind Pug. "Okay, I think that's our cue to go!"

Pug grabbed her successfully this time, but they had only gotten a meter into the air before several bullets pierced his wings and sent them falling to the ground.

Tori scrambled to her feet to try and make a run for it, but one of their attackers were faster and grabbed her from behind. Tori struggled in futility against the strong grip that dragged her into the abandoned church. She cried out and tried to fight back, but the moment she got one of her arms free, another man grabbed it and they both forced her down onto the ground. She let out a cry as she tried to fight back, before getting a hold of her fear and remembering what Cae had taught her these last few months.

With her hopes of not having to hurt anyone dashed, she closed her eyes and let her body fall limp as she opened her eyes to the Walkway. It should have been enough to wake her to an alternate dimension, only now she was in an unknown place that didn't look to be anywhere near the church. Two red eyes looked back at her from the darkness. The uncanny light spread to reveal long, black hair that covered a woman's face. Tori felt as if she should know the woman from somewhere, but she wasn't sure. She wasn't even sure if she consciously saw any of it.

The stranger that hid her face came towards her, and Tori was forced back to the ground again from an invisible strike to her chest. The woman's face was hovering over hers now, and her body was weightless on her, compared to the dark energy that pinned down Tori. "Who are you?" she asked in fear. "What do you want?"

The woman sat up straight, with a smile as if this was all a game, holding a knife in one hand. "By the time this is over, you will remember me Tori. You will remember everything."

Tori woke with a scream when the woman came down on her throat with a knife, only to find that she was standing on her own feet just in time to keep herself from toppling over. She blinked and looked around, not recognizing the alleyway that she was somehow standing in now. One thing for sure wasn't right; as the bodies of the three men who had attacked her at the church were now lying dead around her.

Frozen in shock, Tori looked up as a man yelled at her from the other end of the alleyway. All she could make out of what he shouted was 'demon,' and that was enough to send her feet running the other way down the alley.

She had just made it to the end of it when a police car pulled up and the officer got out of the car, aiming his gun at her.

"Freeze!" he ordered.

Tori did with her hands raised before her, but her mind was still going at full-speed panic. Fight or surrender? There was no slipping back into the Walkway with the woman there and ready to kill her and her current state of panic. If she fought him off, there would be no chance of ever proving that the Institute and Whisper handlers were not the world's enemies. If she surrendered, all was just as lost, as she was the only Hush who could supposedly stop the coming of the end with her command over the Whispers.

Before she could make a choice, Pug made the choice for her, and dropped out of the air right on top of the police car and fanned out his wings at his sides. For a moment he looked like a noseless, infuriated dragon. The car's windows shattered and the cop rolled out of the way just in time to avoid being slashed in two by the gargoyle's giant claws. Pug sprang off of the crushed car then and went straight for Tori. He scooped her up in one arm and was out of the alley and back into the air of the Walkway before she could take in her next breath.

10

THE ATTACK AGAINST the cop in the alleyway should have been enough to send the entire police force down on the school. Yet as Pug flew them to the Institute's rooftop, Tori saw no souls out of place outside of the building. If anything, it was quieter than usual, as even the more devoted protesters were no longer outside of the gates.

Tori had just touched down on the

rooftop when Feather flew up to her and hovered before her in the Walkway. Before she could leave the darkness on her own, someone grabbed her arm and pulled her out of the Walkway by force. "What the--?"

Matthew was standing before her now, and he looked as surprised as she did. "Well hell, it worked."

Tori looked herself over to make sure she was not missing a body part and then looked back at him. "How did you do that?"

"It's as I've calculated. You don't actually up and vanish entirely when you go into the Walkway. You just turn into some kind of spiritual energy in this world, while becoming a physical being in the Walkway."

Tori raised an eyebrow, before ducking when he started to shout at her next.

"Just what were you thinking leaving like that on your own? The news is going completely nuts! They're saying that you murdered three men!"

"I didn't kill anyone. Someone set me up and dropped me from one place to another before those men. I've never seen such power before--it's like they just teleported me there."

"All this happened while you were in the Walkway?"

"Yeah," Tori replied and caught the hovering Feather in her hands. It was impossible for a sparrow to hover like a hummingbird, yet somehow the small Whisper had no trouble doing just that. "I saw this woman too--she was threatening me before she planted me on the other side of the city, where a cop conveniently appeared out of nowhere on top of it all."

"Maybe it's some kind of Wraith

handler power. I mean, they have to be in some sort of close proximity to their Wraiths to command them, and seeing as they are masters of destruction, being able to get out quickly would help too."

Tori thought quietly to herself of how Vincent was able to vanish around her and reappear with little trouble. "So it's an angry Diruo. I suppose I'll stop freaking out now."

"Don't you even think about giving up on us." He said and took Feather from her hands. Matthew now wore the most serious look she had ever seen on his face. "And this running away on your own to save the world, stops now. I don't know what you're looking for out there, but today you went far enough."

"Just how is a crazy Hush supposed to help anyone locked up in this place?" Tori asked, crossing her arms in front of her.

"Are you hurt?"

"No, not unless you include the part where I'm a complete crazy case now, I'm great."

"You must see what's going on here. Tori, you're smarter than you let on. Whoever is setting you up and giving you nightmares is not strong enough to take you head on. They're pushing every button you have and trying to break your spirit and confidence, and then they will likely make their move against us."

Tori sat down next to Matthew on the ledge of the rooftop. "They're strong enough to use me as their puppet. I can knock someone unconscious through the Walkway, but possess someone--that's beyond me."

"Possess? Let's hope the Whispers aren't looking to us as their next hosts..."

"You remember when we talked last in

the cafeteria? I have no memory of walking up from the basement to the caf on my own. This woman--whoever she is-- not only manipulated a scenario where I thought Kenji's Samurai was under her control, but controlled me too."

"Maybe she's just another Hush. Your powers over the Whispers went crazy when Jade first arrived too, which brings me to yet another worry."

"Is Jade alright?" Tori asked with concern.

"I heard her arguing with Kenji the other day," Matthew said as he looked over the side to the ground below. "I stopped next to Jade's door and peeked in, and that's when I saw these rather gross looking black lines on the palms of her hands. Whatever they were, she was fighting with Kenji about them. Any chance you know what they could be?"

"Black lines?" Tori asked, confused.

"I can only assume they aren't good as I already know that your life lines indicate how much time alive you have left."

"What makes you say that?"

"I heard Kenji and Jade mention that as well," Matthew said as he took her right hand and flipped it over to study her palm. Furrowing his eyebrows, he looked her straight in the eyes. "I thought Pug was supposed to be preventing you from losing your life force in the Walkway?"

"He was...until that graveyard Wraith broke him. That's all I have to go on now."

"You have to tell Cae."

"No!" Tori shouted at him and took her hand back. "He has enough to be concerned about as it is. Please, Matthew."

"Like hell I'm just going to sit here and do nothing but watch you slowly die."

"I won't go into the Walkway anymore then. I promise. Just don't tell Cae. Please," Tori begged.

"No more Walkway," Matthew said firmly and raised his finger at her, "or I tell Cae and then I substantially upgrade the birdcage that I'm working on with him for you."

"Alright," Tori said. "But never mind me--what about Jade? Just why would she have black lines on her hand?"

"If she hasn't told you, then it can't be good. Then there is my other current theory."

"Which is?"

"The Wraiths don't seem to have any limit to how much they and the Diruo can mingle in the Walkway. What if these black lines are some sign of stolen life energy?"

"That's crazy--I won't believe that Jade

is a Wraith handler," Tori insisted. "She doesn't have a mean bone in her whole body."

"Then you need to confront her before we leave her in charge here when we visit Whispering Stone. Especially as you said it was a woman who attacked you."

Tori nodded and watched as Matthew closed his laptop and got to his feet.

"I'll research some more on Whispering Stone. Maybe we will make some progress tomorrow. Try and get some rest. I wouldn't be the least bit surprised if this nightmare enemy is capitalizing on the weak state of your mind due to your exhaustion. Cae and I will keep an eye on you in the meantime."

"Thanks, Matthew," Tori said with a faint smile, and he left at that. She sat in silence by herself for a while after. She feared what Cae would have to do to pull her out of the latest mess she had made. She hated herself even more for putting everyone in the Institute at risk of losing what had become their only home from the world of Whisper and Wraith haters outside of it. She lay down on the ledge and closed her eyes, whispering a prayer to the chilly air that she wouldn't be dragged into a nightmarish reality again.

11

TORI FELT LIKE the encounter in the alleyway with the psychotic woman had left a curse on her, as more bad luck arrived at the Institute that afternoon. She looked up from the side of the dry fountain she sat on as the footsteps came to a stop before her. The familiar, smirk face of Kris Fedan from her old high school looked down at her with the same deluded expression of superiority. *You have to be kidding me...* Tori thought to herself. "You really have some nerve showing up here."

"The same could be said about you. Here I was hoping that your building had crushed you."

Tori was on her feet now, as she was not in the mood for having a conversation with this heartless jerk, or wasting any of her limited energy knocking him out. "This is a school for Whisper handlers, and unless by miracle you have obtained the services of one, you need to leave."

"I thought you would never ask," Kris replied and looked back to where there was a rather odd circle of various Whisper statues on the expanse of grass to the side of the driveway. Tori had been pondering them for most of the morning. Of a horse, cheetah, and raccoon, the horse came to life and walked over to them.

"A horse? You sure that one is yours, cause I don't see how it would match with you--unless you account for only its face." Tori gave a brief glance around as Pug wasn't answering her outstretched thoughts. If this horse was a Wraith, she might have to run for her life, yet.

"Laugh while you can, because I haven't forgotten how you humiliated me with that ugly Whisper of yours before." Kris stalled then, as he was likely commanding by thought his horse to trample Tori into the ground. Whatever he was trying to do, it soon became clear that it wasn't working. With her patience all used up, Tori looked at the horse and then focused harder to touch its thoughts. It moved and a massive smile spread across Kris' face. Well, for only a second before his horse Whisper grabbed his shirt between its teeth and flung him down the driveway like a bucket of hay.

Shaking her head, Tori was silently relieved that she still had some grip of her powers over the Whispers. She walked over to where Kris was trying to sit up, looking completely lost as to what just happened. "Well, I suppose since you're new here, I should formally welcome you. Welcome to Four Winds Institute. I am Tori Calas, the Hush of this school. You will be a good boy or I will use my position of authority to personally throw you out of here."

Kris just stared up at her, speechless.

"Oh, and there is one more thing," Tori added gently, before sending her fist straight into his face, hard enough to put him out cold. "Just because my mother and those who died in my building can't hit you themselves."

"Tori!" Cae's voice yelled as he ran out

of the school. He stopped beside her and looked at the new student she had rendered unconscious. "What are you doing!? Have you lost your mind?"

Tori had already thought up a bunch of excuses but settled on a simpler one, "I... I thought he was Wraith handler."

Cae looked at the docile horse Whisper and then back at her. "Seriously?"

"Just look at it," Tori said as innocently as she could, before quietly sneaking around Cae and slipping through the front door of the school for somewhere to hide that did not include the Walkway.

12

CAE PUT HIS car into park after they pulled into the parking lot of what was once the Whispering Stone Institute. He briefly looked back at Matthew before setting his eyes to where Tori stared out the window. "You picking up on anything?"

Tori had yet to be open fired on by him for having knocked out Kris, and the question sounded like a trap. So she kept her answer simple and shook her head.

"After we blew up the Arc, they likely cleared out all the evidence that ever said they were here," Matthew said as he continued to type into his laptop. "But they might have left something behind."

"I guess it's worth a look." Tori opened the door and stepped out of the car and Cae, Kenji, and Matthew did the same.

"The last time we looked inside an abandoned building, we were attacked by ten-foot snakes and nearly killed," Cae reminded them as they walked towards what looked like the front entrance to the place.

"Best out of three?" Matthew joked as he began to try and break the entrance code at the front of the building. It took him several tries, but on the eighth attempt the lock on the door clicked open.

"You're rather good at breaking into

places," Tori said as they went inside.

"Well, I did cheat by asking Feather and all. Combinations are a lot easier to guess when you have a million voices in the Walkway whispering them to you." Matthew caught the tiny sparrow in his hand and lifted her from his pocket to look at her for a moment before putting her back. They walked along the white-walled corridors and looked into one room after the other, in search of something of use.

Tori closed her eyes and tried to make her thoughts heard by Pug, who followed them on the rooftop. Even though he seemed to hear her, he made no effort to voice any kind of response in turn. She wondered if the old Pug would have known anything about this place.

"Looks like this is the center of the building," Cae said as they came to a stop in what might have been a control room once.

Matthew looked around for anything he could plug into, but only bare screens remained. "Well, it was worth a--" He stopped when the monitor suddenly came on by itself.

"What did you do?" Tori asked.

"That wasn't me," Matthew said in his defense and lifted his free hand that wasn't holding his laptop to prove it so.

They all stared at the screen then, but only static could be seen.

Cae looked to ponder on it deeply, before looking at Tori. "Your mother used to work with ESP and what-not, didn't she?"

"Are you suggesting that my mother wants to speak to me from beyond the grave by TV static?" Tori replied.

"She might still be alive," Matthew

added, hoping to lift her darkening mood. "No one found her body."

"No one found much of anything, Matthew," Tori spat back, harsher than she had intended. "A several-ton building crushing everything and everyone into oblivion has that effect."

"Sorry, I didn't mean it like that," Matthew said. "I just think we should remain optimistic that she might still be alive." Then he went off on his own to find something to do somewhere else.

"Matthew--"

Cae caught Tori's shoulder and it had the effect of cooling off her temper, and she already regretted having yelled at Matthew for things he had no part in of her past.

"Not everything is a battlefield, Tori. But you've been acting like there is something bigger going on that you won't tell me."

"I just don't take to stress that well, that's all," Tori said as an excuse.

Cae hugged her and she felt a bit better as she rested her head against his chest. She wondered if his heartbeat would stay the calm, constant beat that it always was should the world decide to fall down around them that very moment. "We should get going before we're caught."

He let her go and she watched him leave, before looking back at the screen when she was alone in the room. Only this time, an unfamiliar face looked right back at her.

Tori's scream had brought Cae, Matthew, and Kenji back into the room on full alert and looking for a threat. They looked back at the screen that Tori stood paralyzed before.

"What did you see?" Kenji asked.

"There was a face--in the static on the screen just now," Tori replied while trying to stop herself from shaking.

"Who was it?" Cae asked.

"I don't know."

Matthew looked over the screen and the wires and machines attached to it and found nothing out of the ordinary. "You sure you didn't see things?"

"Should anything come as a surprise anymore? Seriously, Matthew," she rebuked. "We know the Whispers are spirits that can do things."

"Well, Whispers are real, ghosts have yet to be proven," he replied matter-of-factly.

"Are you kidding me? If spirits leaving their dead world and coming back as Whispers doesn't count as ghosts, I give up. Clearly I brought the wrong mad scientist along for this." Tori sighed and looked at Cae, who looked completely lost on just what to think.

"Whispers possess and move stone around--not electronics. They hate water--heck I can only imagine how much they would hate all the static in this screen. Maybe you're just tired--?" Matthew suggested.

"I am not tired! I know what I saw!" Tori shouted back at Matthew. "Can't you like plug into it and see what's in there?"

"It's dead, Tori. All the machines in here are dead, wiped clean, rusting--or both."

Tori let out a frustrated tight-lipped scream and Matthew threw up his hands in defeat and left her and Cae alone in the room after that.

"Well, whatever it was, it looks like it's gone now. Let's get out of here, just in case this place is haunted," Cae said.

Her mother, father, and Headmaster Deron had worked here once. Now her mother was dead and her father was nowhere to be found. She remembered what the snake had said about the 'God in the Machine.' It had said that it could channel death energy into machines. She went over to the largest screen, and then to the wall that held it up. On finding a small hole, she grabbed the paneling and began to pull piece by rusting piece away.

"Tori, what are you doing?" Kenji asked as he returned to the room.

"Kenji, I need a bit more muscle, this one is...stuck!" Tori said and fell backward when she lost her grip on the sheet metal.

Kenji took hold of it and tried to force it away, but had no luck. "I'll call my Whisper, one moment." A minute later the giant samurai walked into the room, shaking the floor with its weight with its every step. He pointed to the wall and stepped back, but the Whisper made no move to assist him as instructed. He cleared his throat and hit the wall that needed to be removed, but still his Whisper did nothing.

Tori looked for the samurai's mind in the Walkway, before opening her eyes to await it doing as told. It hesitated for a few moments more, before walking closer to the wall and grabbing hold of it. The Whisper pulled it free with one swift motion, then stepped back.

"I'm sorry, Tori. I don't know why my Whisper has chosen now to be uncooperative."

"I think I might understand why," Tori said and pointed at the heavy cables and blinking lights that lay behind the wall.

Matthew and Cae returned to the

room, and could see what Tori and Kenji had found.

"Matthew, that doesn't look like a dead computer to me," Tori said as she looked back at him.

Matthew stepped closer to get a better look inside the wall. "No, it doesn't. But it looks like all these wires not only lead somewhere else, but power something a lot bigger than anything to be found in here."

Tori closed her eyes and looked in the Walkway, in the same direction of the wall. But there she couldn't see any wires; only the dark, rising blackness of the Silence. "It's connected to the Silence--I see nothing but its energy where those wires are."

"Is it using it as a path or what?" Cae asked.

"If it is, I think it might be powering

the God in the Machine."

"Just what is that supposed to be?" Cae asked.

"I don't know. I've just been having nightmares and so far what I can pull from them--if this thing really does exist-- is that it's enslaving the Wraiths and their energy."

"You could have mentioned this before," Cae scolded.

"Until now I wasn't sure it was real," Tori said in her defense.

"Has your dreams said anything of where it might be?" Matthew asked. "Cause there has to be millions of these wires in the city."

"Then there is the other half to what you said," Cae added. "The part about the Wraiths being enslaved. The Silence is one thing, but I can't imagine unleashing the Wraiths on us, either."

"Perhaps that is what is making the Silence so powerful," Kenji suggested.

"What do you mean?" Tori asked, brushing the rest of the dirt and dust off of her pants from her fall.

"The Whispers and Wraiths are souls of once-living people. Souls that to some degree, retain their ability to understand emotions. If someone suddenly started enslaving them, it would make for a lot of angry spirits."

"There is no way we are freeing any of those monsters. If these wires do lead to some all-powerful Machine, then we need to get it under control," Cae said.

"Or we could free them."

"You can't be serious, Tori," Cae said. "They wouldn't waste a moment destroying us."

"Likely, because seeing as these wires are connected to this old Institute, then that could only mean that the research our parents were involved with here has contributed to this Machine of angry Wraiths."

"Well, I don't think getting ourselves killed would fix anything," Cae said and left the room.

Tori let out a sigh and looked at Matthew.

"I have to agree with Cae, Tori. Without you in particular, the Whispers would be destroyed by the Wraiths and the Silence likely has all the power by now to destroy whatever it intends to because of this Machine," Matthew said.

"So you think we will lose no matter what we do?" Kenji asked.

"No, I'm not giving up hope. If we find this Machine we might be able to do something," Matthew replied.

"The Wraiths won't listen to me. If we

find the Machine, we're going to have to find Kali first," Tori grumbled.

"Let's head back then," Matthew said. "If anything, we're going to have to take the Institute's power off of the grid. If this Silence can get into the wires of the school, then all of the students are in danger."

Tori nodded and watched Matthew leave, before looking at Kenji. "What are you thinking, Kenji?"

"I think we should leave this place first, and talk more back at the Institute. I find the energy in this place rather unnerving."

Tori gave one look back at the screen that was black again, then followed after him, trying to rub away the lasting chill on her arms.

13

TORI HESITATED FOR some minutes outside of Headmaster Deron's office. She had no idea how to bring her concerns before him without sounding even crazier than she had already come off as so far. She took in a deep breath and knocked on the door before her, before opening it and heading inside of his office.

"Were you able to find anything at the old Institute?" Headmaster Deron asked as Tori walked in.

"Um... Yes," Tori started, still not knowing how to express what was on her mind to Cae's father. "What we found at the old Institute might suggest that we're in danger from our own power lines."

"What do you mean?" Deron asked.

"I think there is a Machine out there enslaving the Whispers, and the Silence is spreading through the power grid. We have to disconnect the school's electricity as I think it is fueling this Machine that is further fueling the rage of the Silence."

Deron gave a quick laugh before shaking his head. "Tori, what you're asking is impossible. All of our security systems are powered by electricity."

"I know."

"How would we run the kitchen? The elevators? How would we keep the fence up that is keeping the angry public out?"

"I don't know," Tori replied. "But whoever is operating this Machine of dead souls is going to use it against us."

"Have you foreseen this?" the Headmaster asked with concern.

Tori thought on it for a moment before replying, "My visions have been uncertain lately, but what I manage to see of them adds up to this enemy who is not the Diruo. If it continues to expand, it will become completely unstoppable--if it's not that already."

"Tori, I can't cut the power to the school unless you can give me some kind of evidence--or at least your own certainty--that this 'Machine' enemy is real. I have to look to the immediate and real threat right outside our gates."

Tori let out an inner scream as he sounded just like Cae. "The Whispers can defend the gates. If the Silence can get inside the Institute through the grid, it's more of a danger to everyone in the school."

"What do you mean?" the Headmaster asked.

"I think it's strong enough to not only make a mess of my visions, but control to some degree the Whispers as well. First it was Kenji's samurai acting weird, then Cae's lion. My worst fear is that it can set them against us."

"If it is this enemy's intent is to distract you or convince you to drop our only defenses, then it is doing just that. Without our electricity, we won't be able to keep this school up and running. It would not take a Machine then to tear everything we cherish around here apart. So the final answer is no. I'm sorry, Tori."

Tori felt like punching a wall with her frustration, but held it in and left the

Headmaster's office at that. Deron was right, of course. She didn't know what had possessed her to make her think that putting the school in the Dark Ages would save them. Her gut feelings were starting a riot against her reasoning in her head, and she knew that she had to forget about it before she was deemed too crazy for active duty as a Hush.

She was halfway back to her room when she suddenly came to a stop in front of what had once been Vincent's room, before he betrayed the Tueri. She knocked on the door and found it to be still unoccupied, despite the desperate need for rooms with the school's population having exploded over the last few months. She stepped inside the dark room and turned on the lights.

Many of his belongings and clothes were still present exactly as he had left them. Overall he was tidy, and nothing seemed out of the ordinary from a normal teenager's room.

Tori snooped around a bit longer, before stopping at an odd sketch of a snake pinned to the wall over his desk. She looked closer at it and saw that it resembled the one that had been tormenting her with riddles of the 'God in the Machine.' She wondered if Vincent had at some point seen the snake as well. Tori took the sketch down and went over to his bed.

She sat down on his burgundy comforter and closed her eyes. Tori tried to remember everything that the snake had told her before it had--or had not-- been attacked by Kenji's samurai. It had mentioned the Machine enslaving the Wraiths. It had mentioned an open door into the Institute that she had yet to find as the school was sealed off on all sides, so that was likely the power grid. And it had mentioned a woman, which Tori assumed had been the one tormenting her as of late. Then she remembered Pug, and how he had likely lost his voice and the essence of what he was to the Silence. With the snake having not made an attempt to come back, she added it to her list of concerns. Her only lead to the Silence could be lost now.

Then she added all of the past riddles to her newest ones. Four Winds Institute was the last of the Whisper schools that had not been destroyed. At first it had been assumed that the Diruo had done this, but they had made no direct attack against the school. She remembered the men lying at her feet in the alleyway, and how the cop appeared so quickly. How did he know to be there at that exact time?

This enemy not only had the cops in its control, but access to likely whatever it wanted in the city because of the power lines.

A horrifying thought occurred to Tori that if it did put out all the lights and basic services, the city would be fumbling over itself in the dark while the Wraiths would be free to crush them.

Tori sat up with a renewed determination. She had to find this Machine, somehow, even if it meant following every Silence-infused cable she could get her hands on straight to its source.

14

TODAY TORI HAD discovered that next to her ability as a Hush, she also had a uniquely devastating ability to disassemble things.

She stepped back from the wall in the electrical room and admired her handiwork. With the help of the white sphinx that had guarded the Hush before her, she had completely torn away all of the concrete and drywall to reveal the wiring behind.

Tori closed her eyes and opened them back into the Walkway to see what the wires looked like from there. To her surprise, and at the same time relief, there was no dark energy of the Silence to be seen.

She blinked and her vision returned to the basement around her, and she looked at the white sphinx who wore a face of curiosity, likely wanting to know just what she expected to find. "Okay, so the Silence isn't in here, which means there is something I'm missing. Why can it get to any part of the city, but not in here?"

The sphinx had never given any indication that it could speak, but as if to answer her, its head turned to face her with the one of its four that wore a large smile.

Deciding something out of the

creature was better than nothing, she continued the game of charades. "Is it because of me?"

The smiling face continued to face her.

"So I have some kind of superpower over this Silence that I'm not aware of? Great." Then another thought occurred to her; "Is this ability of mine something that can be taken?"

The head of the sphinx rotated and it faced her with its serious, angrier looking expression. Tori took the response as a yes.

"They still have to go through all of us," Cae's voice said from behind her.

Tori cringed at the idea that he was here, and witness to the destruction she had done to the school's wall. "Uh, hey, Cae," she said as she slowly turned to face him.

"I would ask what you're doing, but

judging from the destruction, I can only assume that you're trying to find the Silence in our electrical grid."

"And it's not here," Tori added optimistically.

"Finally some good news then. Well, seeing that this has at least put you in a good mood, I'll capitalize on that."

"What do you need?" Tori asked, gently shoving a large rock aside that was one of the many stacked behind her now.

"I wanted to ask you out for New Year's."

Tori blinked as her mind tried to catch up to what he was talking about. She had expected a thorough scolding, not a date. Certainly not a date during their time of crisis now. "I don't think we should be going anywhere outside of the Institute."

"Oh, we are going out for New Years, whether you want to or not. I already made all the plans and everything."

Tori hated parties. She more or less hated anywhere with more than a handful of people. But she hated disappointing Cae even more, and only starting with her latest madness, she also felt like she owed him.

"Tori, I miss you," Cae said and walked closer to her, before pulling her into his arms. His cinnamon scent remained the same as it always was, and equally intoxicating. "I want to spend some time with you."

Tori took in a deep breath, and his scent and tone suffocated her will that wanted to pry herself out of this predicament. "Where are we going?"

"It's a surprise," Cae replied with his overly soothing tone.

"I hate surprises," Tori mumbled back.

"You'll love this one," Cae said

enthusiastically and kissed her on the head. Then he trotted off like a man with an urgent purpose, before pausing in the doorway. "Oh, did you need any help cleaning this up?"

"No, I got it," Tori replied solemnly and watched him go. She looked at the sphinx who still had its angry face on. It wasn't the only one who thought it was a bad idea to leave the Institute.

When she was done with the majority of the mess in the electrical room, Tori headed back to her room wishing that the job had been enough to exhaust her into not thinking more about heading outside. Creeping slowly to her closet, she dared to look in. She didn't own any dresses, and being a Hush didn't exactly give her a salary to go out and buy one. After her mother was killed and the only home she had before this one was destroyed, everything she owned had been destroyed with it. Next to her school uniform and a few outfits given by classmate friends, she didn't have much. She fell onto her bed and pondered crying until one might magically appear, before getting an idea.

Tori bounced off of her bed and headed down the hall. She found Jade's door slightly ajar and peeked her head inside. She wasn't there, and Tori pondered just barging in and explaining later. The odds of finding something to borrow were against her, as Jade was at least two or three sizes smaller than her. So she decided that she would just have a quick look and slipped inside. The moment she made it to the closet and opened it, Matthew's voice startled her from the door.

"Why didn't you just ask him to take

you out shopping?"

"Matthew, this stalking thing is getting a bit much," Tori replied.

"I wasn't stalking you," Matthew replied and picked up Feather from his pocket, before opening his hand so she could fly to Tori. "She was."

Tori just watched the Whisper sparrow land on her shoulder and let out a sigh.

"Did you find anything in the basement?"

"Absolutely nothing. This Silence supposedly can spread to every corner of the city, but isn't inside the Institute itself. The worrisome faces that Melissa's sphinx has been giving me seems to add up that our current immunity to it has something to do with me." Tori looked back in Jade's closet and took out a couple dresses, before concluding that she would never fit in anything that the other Hush's closet had to offer.

"Yeah, you definitely need to unwind a bit. I'll tell you what; you endure an hour in the computer store with me tomorrow, and I'll tag along to all the clothing stores necessary to find and then buy a dress for you. Deal?"

Tori gently touched Feather on the head, before scooping her up into her hand as if the Whisper were a hamster. "What's in it for you?"

A mischievous grin stretched across his face. "You just let me worry about that."

Tori dropped her head, fearing that whatever plan Matthew had up his sleeve, it was going to include her in a way that she wasn't going to enjoy.

15

TORI WASN'T FEELING much better at
the mall the next day, as shopping wasn't
something that helped her unwind at all.
Matthew had stopped for some quick
coffee for both of them, before continuing
on to his destination with her in tow. Soon
after reaching the computer store, she
came to a stop next to him. Matthew was
staring at the glass banister and the rest of
the mall instead of the store. "Are we

going inside?"

"You see that fat fart over there?" Matthew said as he watched the store from Feather's eyes who had her head stuck out of his pocket like it was her nest.

"Yeah?"

"K, here is the plan. You are going to go in there and say that you are interested in a gaming PC. Something top of the line. Then you are to use your natural cluelessness about computers and ask him everything possible about it. Hard drive, RAM, memory, motherboard--anything and everything to keep his attention on you."

"What makes you think he will be the slightest bit interested in me?"

"Trust me, he will be. I'll give a whistle when it's time to bail."

"Wait--what are you going to do in the meantime?" Tori asked in concern.

"I'm just gonna look around."

"Browsing? Why do I get the feeling you're going to rob the place?" she asked and crossed her arms in front of her.

"I'm not going to steal a thing, I promise. I just want a bit of air to look around. It won't take long. Now get going."

Tori pulled her blond bangs out of her eyes and let out a loud sigh. "If you get us arrested--"

"Hop hop," Matthew insisted and gave her a gentle shove towards the store.

Tori reluctantly headed inside, even as everything told her that this was a really bad idea. She didn't know how many free criminal acts she had left before it would land her in jail.

"Hello, Miss. Anything I can help you with?" the chubby employee asked as he approached her.

Tori looked at the balding guy and pulled her act together. "Actually, yes. I'm looking to buy a gaming computer, only thing is that I don't know much about them."

"Well, I think I can help you with that," he replied politely and showed her to where all the PCs were on display. Tori continued to listen and ask questions, while cautiously glancing to just what Matthew was doing in the other isle. *If he steals anything I swear...*

"If you were looking to spend a bit more money, this one here would be your best bet. It has..."

Tori focused back on the salesman and pretended to be interested. Within a few minutes, Matthew had left and gave the whistle to retreat. She excused herself from the salesman at that and then left the store, catching up with Matthew a few stores down. Looking him over, it appeared that he didn't steal a thing.

"Can I carry your bag for you?"

"Uh...sure..." Tori said and took off her knapsack. He took it from her and then walked to where the washrooms were and past them, until he turned the hall and stopped under a ventilation grate.

Matthew pulled the grate off and set it on the floor, then opened up her knapsack before setting it under the ventilation as if to catch something. Then, one by one, various computer things began to fall out of the vent and into her knapsack.

"Good lord! Seriously, Matthew?" she cried.

He smiled and zipped up her knapsack before putting it onto his back. "You never said anything against Feather stealing. And that was an awesome haul. So, which store are we hunting down your dress in?"

"Here I'm trying to save the world from demons, and I'm stealing with one!"

"Hey, I would have no problem paying for it, but the guy in there has been a complete jerk to me since the day I first walked into that store. That and everything is overpriced."

"And where would you get that kind of money?" Tori demanded to know.

"After you sent my parents fleeing from the Institute, they came to their senses a few weeks later and remembered that I'm there son and not a profitable investment. I suppose some part of them feels less guilty by sending me some money--heck if I know or care the whys to it."

Tori looked at her coffee in her hands as she remembered the day that his parents had almost taken Matthew just so that they could give him to the Diruo.

What she had done was brash at the time, but ultimately she was left without regret. "I can't believe you... Just for that, I'm stopping by the lingerie store as well so I might forget all this!"

Matthew's face turned so red at that his freckles vanished entirely. But he didn't argue as he followed after her to his execution by embarrassment.

16

TORI DIDN'T KNOW how long she had stared at herself in the mirror, only that no amount of staring would make the dress she was wearing go away. It was not to say that she didn't like the simple black garment, it just didn't feel like she was looking at herself anymore.

"Cae will love it, now stop worrying so much. Today is supposed to be fun," Jade insisted as she finished pinning all the wayward strands of Tori's blond hair up. "What's the worst thing that can happen? You have some fun?"

"We both have very different ideas of what is fun," Tori replied, finding that it was impossible to keep her bitter mood to herself.

"No, we don't. You're just depressed." Jade took Tori's arm and spun her around. "Perfect." She went over to Tori's bed and got her coat for her. "Now off with you. Cae is already downstairs and waiting."

Tori had scripted a whole novel of excuses of why this was a bad idea, but knew that none of her lines would work on Jade.

"I will keep everything under control while you're gone. You have a phone?"

Tori shook her head and then looked at her door where Matthew flipped one open in his hand.

"I didn't forget about you." He smiled and then stuffed the phone into her purse. "It has everybody's number already programmed into it."

"And let me guess, a tracking device and an elaborate trap shrouded in the deception of fun?" She didn't add that this phone was likely one of the things that he had stolen from the mall with the help of Feather.

"Tracking device, yes. Trap, no," Matthew answered.

Tori sighed. "Thanks." She took her purse from Matthew and left her room.

"Go get him," Matthew added with a mischievous grin.

Tori shook her head in hopelessness. She felt like a doll all dressed up and powdered for the slaughter. Then she reminded herself that she would be with

Cae and that it wouldn't be anything like that. Assuming she could momentarily forget that all the world's shadows were currently trying to kill her.

She reached outside and looked at the driveway that circled in front of the Institute and to where Cae's car was parked. Leaning against it was her man and dressed to kill. He wore a pressed pair of gray slacks and a matching blazer and a white shirt complete with a tie. Tori walked over to him and they both just stared at each other as if looking at one another for the first time.

"Wow. You look amazing."

"Just how the hell am I supposed to keep other women off of you with you looking like that?" Tori countered in a tone that was more of concern than a compliment.

He laughed and then shrugged. "I still

have that tattered school uniform of yours--"

"Don't go there," she scolded him, remembering when Cae had rescued her by jumping in front of a subway train bound to flatten her. Fortunately, her school uniform had suffered the fatality instead of her. The smile on his face suggested that he wanted her to remember just that, too. He likely saw it as a heroic effort on his part, where she still recalled it as one of the few times she had been so helpless. Tori briefly glanced towards the school's gates expecting a mob to be waiting for them to leave, but was surprised when she saw no one. "How did you get rid of the mob?"

"Oh, them? Nothing too dramatic, I promise," Cae assured her, and nodded in the direction of his over-sized lion Whisper, who sat outside of the gate.

Then he opened the passenger side of the car for her to get in.

Tori did and he closed the door before going around and getting in himself. "So do I get to know where we're going yet?"

Cae grinned as he started up his car. "I said it was a surprise. Now be patient."

Tori took in a deep breath and tried to do just that as he drove them away from the school grounds and in the direction of downtown. She told herself to relax and to try and have fun and that her impending madness was likely a result of her being stressed out to the max. Taking a deep breath, she looked at Cae when he set his right hand down on her leg.

"You alright?" he asked.

"Yes," Tori replied, mustering the best fake smile that she could bear to wear. "Though I'm still concerned about this surprise."

Cae returned his hand to the steering wheel as his smile broadened.

Tori got the feeling that it was going to be a very long night.

17

THE LOUD MUSIC was what bombarded Tori's senses first, making it hard to see what might be watching them as they walked up to the club. When they were let in without having to stand in line, any chance of her being able to run away was lost.

They went downstairs and it soon became clear that she had walked into an uncountable number of people. Most danced and jumped to the electronic music with little to no space left between them, and at the end of the room the DJ could be seen playing the music in tune to the flashing spotlights. They may as well have been prison lights for how Tori was quickly feeling imprisoned by the countless number of people around her.

Her head felt like it would explode, if her heart didn't give out first from the bass' heavier beats. How Cae had thought that she would like this place in the slightest was beyond her.

She took in a deep, hot breath as she was already beginning to sweat, and let Cae drag her to wherever he intended to drag her. She was more pleasantly surprised to find that there was a private booth upstairs reserved for them both. It was less crowded, but still loud. Either way, this she could tolerate better as she sat next to him on the leather sofa.

"So what do you think?" Cae asked hopefully.

"I'm thinking how I don't drink," Tori replied, then stopped speaking altogether to avoid saying what she was really thinking.

"Heh, I know that. If it makes you feel better, I didn't bring you here for the music. I wanted you to meet someone."

"You're going to have to be more specific," Tori said and reached for the bucket with a bottle of vodka in it. She contemplated getting drunk to potentially loosen her up enough to take on this night, before stopping when someone's form blocked out the lights and cast a shadow over her in its place. She looked up to find an older woman with her brown hair in a tight bun looking back down at her. There was something about her brown eyes that cause Tori to stare as if she remembered her from somewhere.

"You must be Tori," the woman said first, breaking Tori out of her stupor.

"Uh, hi," Tori replied. Suddenly she remembered that she didn't have an ID or the age to be in this place, and there was now a uniformed cop next to her. She looked back at Cae, fearing he had turned on her or something equally as ludicrous.

"I'm Astella Hean," she said holding her hand out to shake Tori's, "Cae's mom."

Tori melted like ice thrown on a bonfire in relief. She shook the woman's hand and watched Astella sit down on the leather sofa in front of them. Tori hit Cae with her elbow as he continued to giggle under his breath from her reaction, and swore she would beat him bloody later.

"You don't have to worry, Tori. I'm not

here to arrest you or anything. I'm a murder investigator and was hoping that you could give me some insight as to what happened the other night," Astella said.

"I wish I could, but I'm still trying to figure that out myself," Tori replied, truthfully. She looked at Cae then, unsure of just how much of the Whispers' world his mother knew about.

"She knows everything. It's how we've managed to keep the school up and running this long," Cae explained. "My mom has been helping put out fires along with others in the police, FBI and various organizations that are on our side. The government would see us all arrested, but they have no control over the hidden, high concentration of the very people they would see arrested working for them."

"We have help?" Tori asked suspiciously.

"There are many adults in these organizations and places of power who are also Whisper handlers like yourself. It's not a gift limited only to the younger generation. Until recently, it has been rather quiet, but with your appearance, we think there is something bigger and more dangerous out there," Astella continued. "This 'Silence' isn't just a wildfire of death energy--someone is controlling it."

"Do you know who?" Tori asked.

"No, but whoever or whatever it is, it has taken a great deal of interest in you. It's trying to indirectly take you out of the picture. I don't think you look like the type of girl to murder anyone, let alone three men twice your size."

Tori thought back to when they attacked the Arc, and the security she had attacked there, likely killing them or putting them into comas. Either Cae's mom was going soft on her or Cae himself didn't stop to realize just yet that his girlfriend had the power to snuff out souls from within the Walkway. Straightening up, she focused her thoughts back to the present conversation. "Whatever it is, it had its chance to kill me," Tori pondered aloud.

"We need you to use all your resources--the kids of the school if you can for that matter--in finding this threat before it spirals out of control. I don't know how much longer we can protect you. Tori, is there anything else about the Hush that Cae, and myself in turn, doesn't know?" Astella asked.

Tori forced herself not to look at her hands at the question. They already knew that looking into the Walkway took away years of your life. A means to measure it couldn't add anything here but more worry to Cae. She thought back then to the 'God in the Machine' and said its name aloud.

"What is that?" Astella asked.

"Supposedly it's something that can take the Silence's energy and channel it into machines--maybe even contain it-- and it can enslave Wraiths. The machine that Kali was hooked up to looked to be just that, but it wasn't."

"It might have been a smaller version," Astella replied. "Then you and the Tueri took out the Arc and to our knowledge, Kali no longer has that Machine."

"So we should focus more on finding this Machine then?" Cae asked, rejoining the conversation.

"It's a place to start," his mom replied.

Tori looked over the balcony to the dancing people below, and let her mind think back to her fight with Kali, and what she had said to her then;

"You will never win! If you kill me, then you will become me! Nothing will stop what we have started!" Maybe her stalker was looking to become the replacement that Kali was talking about.

"Tori?" Astella asked.

"Huh? Oh, sorry, I was just drifting back into thought to see if I missed anything. Sorry, but I can't remember anything else that might be useful."

"Alright, then I'm off. Cae, keep me updated, and watch out for Tori."

"I will, Mom," Cae said and watched Astella go. He looked back at Tori.

"Your mom seems like a really nice person," Tori said when Astella was gone.

"She's cool."

"What happened between her and your dad?"

"I think it was a matter of pursuing

different interests, and not giving enough time to each other. They're both overly obsessed with their work. My dad doesn't say much on the topic. She left when I was still small."

"I see," Tori replied.

"Well, I know it's not the most romantic New Year's present, but I thought that giving you some hope might cheer you up a bit. That and this was the safest place with all its noise for a bunch of Whisper enthusiasts to carry out a conversation."

"Be a criminal for free ticket from the police? That's like a lifetime of gifts in one." Tori turned and looked at Cae when he laughed, and he looked pleased that he had found a way to make her smile. He set a hand down on the side of her face, and then his fingers drifted down to her neck and behind it. His fingers pulled on the strands of hair that had escaped the countless bobby pins Jade had placed. His touch was warm and comforting, and enough to pull her entire focus onto him and away from the people and noise around them. She inhaled his breath of warm cinnamon and kissed him as his lips came for hers. Tori wrapped her arms around his neck and pulled him closer, stealing every perfect moment that was given to her, until they were both forced apart by breathlessness.

She rested her head against his chest then, as he wrapped his strong arms tightly around her, taking in the scent of her hair. Saving the world could wait, she wanted this moment for herself.

"We'll make this end and you won't have to be scared anymore. No one will." He let go of her and pulled her blond bangs out of her eyes for her. "Now I want to show you something. Your real New Year's gift."

Tori looked at him quizzically, having had enough surprises for one day. Despite that, she got up and followed him to the stairs that led to the roof.

18

TORI LOOKED OVER the side of the rooftop of the club and to the people below. Some were having a smoke or talking with their friends, completely oblivious to just how much time they might have left on this world. She jumped when Cae suddenly grabbed her and held her close, before relaxing when he rested his chin on her shoulder.

"There aren't any Wraiths or Diruo

here, Tori. I have like every spare Whisper keeping an eye on us."

"Isn't that supposed to be my job?" Tori asked.

"No, you just have to remember that you're the emergency override."

Tori shook her head a bit and Cae laughed as he hugged her tighter. "So what did you need to bring me all the way up here for?"

Cae turned his sights to the corner of the rooftop, where a giant pair of eagle Whispers sat in stone. One came to life from his focused thoughts on it, and its gray feathers puffed out around it for a moment. The eagle walked over to them and he set his hand on it and kept his other arm around Tori.

"I already know your little spying secret," she said. Tori watched as he continued to close his eyes and send his thoughts to the eagle until she could sense that he was watching her through the bird's eyes.

"Ah, but you have never tried it yourself," he replied with a devilish grin.

Tori thought about the idea of flying on her own for a moment, then set her hand on the eagle's face.

"You have to clear your mind for it to work," Cae instructed. "You're too used to Pug doing everything for you. This Whisper requires a bit of effort on your part."

Tori tried to clear her mind, but was failing miserably. Happy and calm thoughts, that was all that she needed. That was the only thing she didn't have.

"Remember when you were practicing with Pug as the 'hamster ball?'"

Tori did, and she smiled at the memory of when Cae unlocked the believability of this whole world of Whispers, all by giving her a snow globe with a miniature Pug in it. It was enough to clear her mind and she opened her eyes to find herself in the Walkway--only it wasn't just the Walkway--but the view that the eagle Whisper saw from its eyes.

She dared to look down and found that she hadn't just taken over the eagle's eyes, but its body as well. Then she felt for and stretched her wings and if she could have smiled in the form she was in, she would have.

"Matthew said that we should build you a bird cage first, but I trust that you will come back. You will come back, right?"

Cae's voice was slower and almost impossible to make out, but Tori could hear him. She wondered how Pug was able to decipher hearing people talk like this all the time. Stretching her wings, she flapped a few times until she was able to generate enough lift to fly up and off of the rooftop, before settling back down.

"You sure this is a good idea without building that bird cage I suggested, first?" Matthew asked as he joined them on the rooftop.

"How in blazes did you get into the club?" Cae asked and looked at him.

"Mad skills, what can I say," Matthew said, outstretching his arms to his sides. "That and the bouncer had a small issue with something on his car."

Cae shook his head and looked back at Tori, who looked to be still getting used to how slow their voices were heard in the Walkway. He held her human body a bit tighter as an assurance that he wouldn't let anything happen to her if she did decide to go for a flight. "Now go and get your need to take on the city and find the source of the Silence, and come right back, got it? No leaving the bird," he instructed her, as if she were now a child again.

Tori was happier with the idea of both of them watching her body, and in a rush of wind took to the air and climbed much higher this time.

"What if she doesn't come back?" Matthew asked in concern.

"She will. Besides, I made sure I did this with her hungry."

They both laughed at that and watched as Tori vanished into the clouds that darkened the glow of moonlight.

19

FLYING WAS FUN, and Tori was getting too good at it too fast. Suddenly the idea of protecting her home city or the world for that matter, didn't seem like such a daunting task with how small it all looked from how high she was now.

She was learning more about the Whispers like this too. Her eagle felt no exhaustion, felt no need for air and was never cold or hot. It was starting to make sense why they would take possession of stone now over anything else, or anything living. Stone had a certain immortality quality to it and with how emotionless they were, they would feel nothing like this. In more ways than one, Whispers were the ultimate freedom from every kind of pain.

Tori focused on landing and flew closer to the Earth until a concentrated force of the dark energy of the Silence caught her attention. She changed direction and landed on top of the building that was its source. She could hear a lot of shouting and looked down and inside the glass roof window to see the soul sparks of several people fighting it out. The gunfire was unmistakable, and so was Vincent's voice. A quick count proved that he was outnumbered by the shooters and that his chimera Whisper was nowhere in sight.

She stepped onto the glass of the rooftop and it broke, sending her falling to the floor below. Catching most of her fall with her wings, she spun around on landing and threw the attackers against the ground. Then she looked back at Vincent and could see that he was trying to control her. It took him a few moments to realize that the Whisper that had dropped in on his fight was already well in control by her. He gave up and made a run for it, and she crushed down a brick wall to escape back to the outside, and then took back to the air.

She found Vincent again soon enough and followed him until he had lost his attackers and taken shelter on a different rooftop. Tori nearly stopped flying when he looked right up to where she was hovering and watching him. Figuring that he likely had used his sight of the Walkway to see just who had saved his ass, she sucked up her courage and landed on the rooftop near him.

"Heh, so Cae showed you his little trick. I could never get him to teach me it," he said with a confident smug look on his face.

How could you see that it was me? Tori thought to herself.

"I've only got one guardian angel last time I checked. Though, an eagle totally suits you too. Thanks for saving my hide."

You're welcome. But who were those guys trying to gun you down?

"Eh, there are a few gangs trying to get the most power by getting the most Whisper and Wraith handlers on their side. I told them where to take their offer to recruit me and they didn't take to my answer very well. So...how are things going at the school?"

Fine, for now. Where's your new groupie club?

"About as busy as me. Were you interested in helping out?"

No, Tori replied flatly and spread her wings to leave.

"Wait!" Vincent called and rushed at her. He caught her beak with his hands and tried to hold her still.

What are you doing? Let go of me before I peck your eyes out.

"Where did you leave your body?"

Like I'll tell you that.

"No, I mean *who* did you leave your body with?"

Yeah, this conversation is over. Tori had only managed to take a step back and away from him when a surge of pain shot through her and sent her oversized Whisper body toppling to its side.

"Tori!"

Tori tried to keep her eyes open, as Vincent kept trying to call her back from what felt like death taking her away from him. Then everything went black.

20

TORI DIDN'T KNOW how long she had blacked out for when she finally came around. A faint light caught her attention in the darkness that surrounded her, and she looked to where it came from. She got to her feet and began walking towards it. The moment she was next to it, it vanished and then glowed in a different place in the distance. Tori followed it again, and again until it finally came to a stop and began to expand, revealing what looked like a little girl in the center of the room.

The child's hair was a golden blond like Tori's, and she looked to be crying from where she sat on her knees with her face in her hands.

"Are you alright?"

The girl sat up straight with a start, before scattering back and away from Tori. "Who are you?"

"My name is Tori," she replied simply. "Who are you?" She crouched down to get eye to eye with the little girl.

"Yvon," she replied and wiped a tear away from her light blue sky eyes.

Tori looked hastily around, before looking back at the girl. Was this her sister who had died years before she was born? She remembered that Kali had mentioned something about all the anxieties in her mind being pathways to her downfall, and figured that all her thoughts about her sister had created this scenario before her. Or she had finally lost her mind.

"Is dad with you?" the girl asked.

Tori shook her head. "What is this place?"

"They call it the 'Silence.' I should have listened to that gargoyle--but I didn't and now I can't find my way out."

The idea that her sister's soul had been trapped in such a dark prison for so long made Tori's stomach crawl.

"Can you help me get out of here?" Yvon asked.

"I don't know," Tori replied. Her sister's body would have long decomposed by now, and if she did manage to find a way to free her sister from here, that only left the afterlife for her spirit. If there was any kind of afterlife aside from the Silence. Then there was a very real possibility that she was doomed to be trapped here forever just like Yvon. Deciding to change that subject, she looked back at the little girl with a confident, false smile. Giving up wasn't an option. "What were you looking for in here?"

"The gargoyle said that the only way to stop the Silence was to get all the gargoyles to return. But they won't listen to me and go back."

"Go back? What do you mean?" Tori asked.

"The gargoyles were the ones who were keeping the Silence from spreading. But they stopped doing that and now the Silence is spreading everywhere," Yvon elaborated.

"Why did they leave it?"

"I don't know," the little girl replied.

"So you're saying that if we get the gargoyles to go back to the Silence, it can be what? Contained?"

"I think so. Do you know who they are listening to now?"

Tori stood up. "I have one, and some are with the Diruo. We have to get out of here if we are to get them back," Tori said. She wrapped her arms tightly around her as she thought about Cae and whether he was looking for her. There was enough guilt in her now to trap her here forever.

"Are you alright?" Yvon asked with concern, getting to her own feet.

"Yeah," Tori replied, lying as best she could again. In truth, she was the last thing from it. Somehow she had to pretend to be strong. It was all she had to work with now.

21

TORI WASN'T SURE if what she was staring at was real or not. Here, where time itself seemed to have no meaning of any sort, she could have easily used more time than she ever intended simply to study what was before her. "Who is this?"

"This is the last gargoyle left here," Yvon explained, and then looked back up at the creature that was as big as a six-story building, and a monument of stone onto itself.

Tori wondered if it was alive at all. "Does he talk?"

"Sometimes. Ask him something," her sister suggested.

Tori looked around briefly for just which question of her millions to start with. She decided to start with her predicament. "Hey, big guy, is there a way out of here?"

The ground shook as one of the gargoyle's clawed-hands came free of the stone ground under them. Then its yellow eyes shone down on them and put them into its spotlight.

"Why do you want to leave? What you sought is right beside you," the thunderous voice replied.

Tori waited till her heart stopped vibrating before looking at Yvon beside her. "I have to get back to help my friends.

I have to stop the Silence."

The gargoyle laughed and the light from its eyes went out for a moment as it gave a slow blink. "There is no stopping the Silence. As Yvon has told you, I am the last gargoyle left, and I alone cannot hold it back. There is nothing that can stand in its way now."

"What if the gargoyles came back?"

"It is too late. Even if every single gargoyle were to return, the Silence has spread too far and too fast to stop now. Stay here and keep your soul in peace with the sister you love. The souls of the angry dead will reach out for vengeance, and here you are not in their path."

"I can't stay here! I won't! You have to let me out!" Tori screamed at the gargoyle, but its eyes and the light from them left her and returned to looking straight ahead and into the empty darkness that spanned forever.

"You're my sister?" Yvon asked.

"I think I am," Tori replied, uncertain of everything there was now.

"You won't leave me here sister, will you?" Yvon pleaded.

Tori felt a piece of her heart fall to the floor and shatter with what little light there was around them. "You've been here for over sixteen years, Yvon. Your body is gone."

Yvon sniffled a sob and then looked to the side and the ground. "It has been that long? I never wanted to sleep that long. Why didn't anyone wake me up?"

"They tried," Tori replied, remembering what the Headmaster had told her. "But you had gone too far away."

"If I'm really dead, then I don't want you to die," Yvon replied and wiped the tears from her eyes. "You have to get out of here!"

"I know. I'm trying," Tori replied and looked up at the massive gargoyle in disgust with how it was proving to be completely useless.

"Do they miss me?" Yvon asked.

"Huh? Yeah, they miss you still," Tori replied.

"And Mom?"

"Mom?" Tori forced her tears back as she remembered her building crumbling down on them. The Wraiths had killed their mother. "Especially Mom," Tori assured her.

"You're lying. I heard Mom's voice not too long ago. She sounded like all the other dead souls do--lost. Why won't you tell me what happened to her?"

Tori bit her lip as she tried to piece together in her mind just how to tell a little girl how an entire building fell on their mother. "The Wraiths brought down the whole building on her. If I had been faster to react on my instincts, I might have been able to save her."

Yvon began to cry and Tori hugged her, trying to give the little sister she never had a chance to meet until now whatever comfort she could. "I won't let it end here."

"You have to get the gargoyles back. You said you had one--will the Diruo return theirs?"

Tori remembered all the infuriated gargoyles that had attacked her when they waged a war against the Arc. "I doubt it."

"Then you have to kill their Hush and order them to come back!"

Tori closed her eyes, remembering when she had almost killed Kali, Vincent's sister. Kali had warned her that she would become her if she killed her. But what made her even more fearful was what she would become if she killed her latest attacker who was manipulating the Silence. That was someone she did not want to become. "I need my real Pug back if I'm to be able to do anything. He was attacked by a Wraith and hasn't spoken since."

"Then let's go find him," Yvon said and led the way further into the darkness around them.

22

TORI DIDN'T KNOW how it was possible to fall asleep inside the Walkway, but when she woke again, she found a blindfold made of white lace lying crumpled before her eyes. Curiously she reached for it and examined it from where she lay on her side. It looked like the lace that Melissa, the former Hush of the Four Winds Institute, had left her. Tori wondered if the woman was somewhere around this place, roaming around as well.

She sat up and looked around, and found that Yvon was nowhere to be seen. Worry began to quickly build up in her, and she got to her feet just as her sister's voice called out to her from behind. "Yvon. What's wrong?"

"This is bad--it's the last gargoyle--it's trying to leave!"

"What? Why and how?" Tori asked and sprung towards Yvon.

"I don't know, but we have to stop it!"

Tori ran after Yvon, and just like her sister had said, the massive gargoyle was on the move. "It must be the Silence's Hush calling him."

"How will we get him back? We can't even get the other ones back!" Yvon replied in a panic.

Tori's eyes caught a glimpse of the

white blindfold again, and this time it was floating in the air beside them both. Then, without warning, it darted off and Tori and Yvon wasted no time chasing after it. Two yellow eyes caught her attention from the expanse of the darkness and they weren't Pug's. She ran and didn't stop until she had reached the source of the eyes. It turned out to be Vincent's chimera, and it was now holding the blindfold in between its lion's teeth.

She reached for it, but the giant lion with a scorpion's tail ran off. "Wait!" Tori cried after it, and tried to chase it down, but it had vanished. Frantic, she looked back to see the blindfold on the ground now. It glowed like a ribbon of hope. A hope that just might lead her out of here.

She jogged over to it and snatched it up, not wasting a moment to tie it around her eyes in the hopes that it had some kind of power to save her and her sister. She waited. She waited longer and then longer, until an eternity seemed to pass without anything happening. Tori's eyes swelled up into tears and she collapsed to her knees. Her hands fell to the floor to keep her upright, and her heart felt like it would cave in at any moment. Only it wouldn't get a chance to as a hand touched the top of her head.

Tori snapped her head up, then froze entirely when someone caught her chin in hand and kissed her. She took it in like a desperate breath for life, before pulling away on realizing that it wasn't like Cae's kiss. She pulled off her blindfold and looked at Vincent, who seemed to be as surprised as she was.

"Shoot--that should have been enough to snap you out of here before you kick the crap out of me."

Tori quickly glanced to her sides to confirm that she was still trapped in the Silence, then furrowed her eyebrows at him in anger. "Vincent?"

"Sorry, I'm not the knight in shining armor that you were expecting. But hey, dark knights can totally be heroic in my opinion," he said as he stood up straight.

"What the hell do you think you're doing?" Tori demanded.

"Trying to rescue you, Beautiful. And I don't mean to try and re-enact a fairy tale with you in it or anything, but we should be back in the real world by now." Vincent lifted her hands and then checked her ankles, as if looking for some invisible shackle that was tying her here. Then he looked up to the light blue eyes that weren't Tori's, but looking at him all the same.

"Get away from my sister you evil

Wraith!"

"What the?" was all that Vincent could muster to say before a wave of dark energy reversed the gravity from under him and then hurled him across the darkness of the Silence.

"Yvon, don't!" Tori insisted and then ran to where Vincent had landed.

He lay on his back, seemingly contemplating the vast Silence above him more than any injuries he might have. "Ow. I always knew a girl would kill me one day, but why does it have to be a brat?"

"Can you get us out of here?" Tori asked.

"We'd be out of here by now if your Mini-Me weren't trying to kill me. Tori, this is going to be hard to accept, but your sister is dead and that power she just whipped me with is what's keeping you stuck to this place for the dead."

"Why should I trust you over her?" Tori asked.

"Because I love you, and I would never do anything to hurt you," Vincent replied flatly.

"And pointing a gun at Cae's head isn't hurting me?"

Vincent closed his eyes and let out a long sigh. "I threatened him to save my sister, and I did it because I wouldn't have it in me to threaten you. Yvon is keeping you here, Tori, and it is your regret that is fueling her strength to do so."

Tori studied the truth from his face for a moment, before looking back at her sister who stood just behind her.

"He's lying! It's a trap and he wants you to abandon me here!" Yvon cried back at her.

"We have to bring her with us," Tori

insisted, looking back at Vincent.

"Tori, she is DEAD. And you're going to be dead soon too if we don't get the hell out of here," Vincent said with less patience and got to his feet.

Yvon lifted her hand to strike him down again, but Tori stood in front of Vincent.

"Stop it! Both of you!" Tori shouted, aiming her rising rage at Vincent.

"This is getting ridiculous," Vincent said angrily to Yvon, "and your innocent gig is really bad. You can't have her, so back off." Vincent summoned his chimera to him, and the large creature took up position behind Yvon.

"We have a bigger problem right now!" Tori said and pointed to the massive gargoyle that would soon be impossible to find in the darkness.

"Where is it going?" Vincent asked

Tori, never entirely taking his eyes off of Yvon.

"In all likelihood to the Silence's Hush. If she gets a hold of a creature that big, there won't be any way to stop her."

Vincent focused back on Yvon then, as the little girl suddenly vanished.

"She said that all the gargoyles have to come back--that their absence is what is allowing the Silence to spread. You have to convince your sister to order her gargoyles back here."

"If she does that, our control over the Wraiths will be lost. The Wraiths and Whispers are our only defense, Tori."

"Then I will have to kill her. And this time I will."

Vincent took a step back, and then looked to his side as Yvon appeared again. "I can't let you do that."

"Then leave me here and go," Tori said

and looked at Yvon.

"I'm not going to do that either. There is another way. There is always another way, but your sister--this place is draining all your hope of one. Call Pug and let's get out of here. Together," Vincent pleaded.

Tori shook her head and took a step away from him.

"Call Pug and let's go, Tori! You're not a coward and I refuse to see you become one because of the regret that you cling to. We all make mistakes and we all have regrets, but what happened to your sister happened long before you were even born!"

Tori covered her ears, trying to block all the voices in her head that had taken over now. This was true madness--being unable to think of anything on your own without being crushed by the thoughts of another. In her terror, she cried out Pug's name. In moments, the voices subsided and then came to a stop altogether.

Tori dared to look up, and saw Pug standing on all fours and looking down at her. "Pug?"

The gargoyle moved the wings at his sides a bit, then picked her up into his arms as he took the weight of himself onto his hind legs.

"Sister, no! Please don't leave me!" Yvon cried out to her.

"I'll send all the gargoyles back, sister. You won't be alone much longer."

Yvon fell to the ground as her tears shattered the darkness around Tori and Vincent like glass, releasing them from the Silence in the Walkway and back into the world of the living. Tori found herself flat on her back, staring at the overhead light that blinded everything else around her.

"Welcome back," Vincent's familiar voice said from her side.

"Where am I?" Tori asked as she sat up and gave a better look around to what seemed like a hospital room that she was in.

"Well, I'd say you're in Hell, but that wouldn't be accurate. Welcome to Hades," Vincent explained.

Tori didn't know what he was talking about, let alone how a hospital room might be found in his description. She closed her eyes to get a quick Walkway explanation of where she was, before realizing that she couldn't retreat her consciousness into it. "Exactly where am I again?"

"The Diruo headquarters," another voice said from the open door.

Tori looked at the tall, blond man who seemed just as calm and ignorant to the world around him as Vincent was.

"Who is that?" she asked in her rising concern that only started with being in the base of her enemy.

"I think you should ask him yourself," Vincent suggested.

Tori didn't like the idea or the man, but she pulled together some more of her failing courage for the second time that day. His hauntingly familiar blue eyes were what unnerved her the most.

"That was rather impressive how you handled yourself in the Silence," the man said, then pulled his hands out of his long, gray coat's pockets.

"Thanks, I think," Tori replied.

The man glanced briefly at Vincent, then looked back at her. "I suppose I should introduce myself," he said as he held out a hand for her to shake. "I'm Philip Calas, your father."

Tori was unable to so much as think of shaking his hand as she suddenly felt very lightheaded.

23

"SHE FAINTED. UP until now I didn't think it was possible for her," Matthew said.

"Tori never saw her dad before, and she just finished flying and fighting off those thugs, and god knows where she was when she was in the Walkway. Everyone has their limits," Cae's voice trailed off with his words.

"She was with me," Vincent's voice

added to the conversation.

"And just what were you doing the whole time the Institute was burning down? Keeping her occupied and away from us?" Cae asked angrily.

"No, her sister was keeping her occupied. I was getting her out of there before she could end up spending sixteen years in timeless darkness like Yvon has been," Vincent said in his defense.

"Yvon is dead," Cae replied, frustrated.

"And where do you think the dead go, genius?" Vincent spat back.

"Well, if what Vincent says is true, I think we can officially add angry ghosts to our esoteric dictionary," Matthew mumbled. "But if Yvon is really dead, her body is still missing."

Tori opened her eyes to find Matthew, Cae and Vincent talking not far from the bed she lay on. Remembering that one of them mentioned fire, she sat up fast.

"Easy, you still need to rest," Cae said as he prepared himself to catch her should she choose to spring off of the bed and straight out of Hades.

"Is the Institute okay?" Tori asked.

"It was just a mild fire," Cae assured her.

"If you count a quarter of the school being burned down, sure, it was mild," Matthew added.

"What!?" Tori shouted back.

"Matthew!" Cae snapped at him.

"I don't think hiding things behind her back is going to work," Matthew replied plainly, and then looked at Tori. "That and if you don't want to find your dad anymore, you better let us know, quick-like too."

"Why?" Tori asked as she rubbed her eyes, trying to keep up with everything around her that was happening just too fast. Then it all crashed to a stop on remembering her encounter with her father.

"Because your dad has offered to take us in," Cae finished for Matthew.

"Take us in? Take us where?" Tori asked, completely confused. When none of them answered, she got to her feet and went to the window. Only, it wasn't a window to the outside world, but some kind of massive underground facility. The dark buildings would have been inconceivable from the shadows on the stone walls if it were not for the dim lights in the streets that shaped them. "Holy cheese. Where are we?"

"Underground," a newly familiar voice said.

Tori turned around and found her father standing there. She had wanted to rub him off as a crazy illusion before, but now there was no denying that he was real. He wore a rugged white shirt that had long outlived its brightness and blue jeans. If he was posed to look like a scientist, he only pulled it off somewhat.

"Welcome to my facility, also known as Hades," Philip Calas said with a tone of authority.

"Seriously? Should I keep my eyes on the lookout for Lucifer while I'm here?" Tori replied bitterly and crossed her arms in front of her.

Philip looked at Cae. "Could my daughter and I have a few minutes alone?"

Cae looked at Tori in concern.

"It's fine. If he wanted me dead, he had his chance when I fainted," Tori replied. She felt like she would never be able to live that one moment of weakness in her life down.

"I'll be outside with Matthew," Cae said and left the room after Vincent, closing the door behind them.

Tori was left without any words to say to the man she had wondered about her whole life. All she knew was that her heart was filled with more contempt for him than anything else. He had left her mother because she was born. He was in league with the Wraiths, and she couldn't evade the thought that he likely hated her as much as she hated him.

Philip walked over to her and looked out the window. "It's taken some years to build this place."

"I bet. The government looks like it has been most generous."

"Well, not all things last forever," he replied and looked at her. "When you and your companions sunk the Arc, you gave them an excuse to end our funding. Now, with the world threatened by the Silence, Hades is mostly run by volunteers."

"You must be so proud being the leader of the same people who killed my mother," Tori added in a bitter tone.

"Is that what you think?" Philip asked and looked at her with his emotionless pale blue eyes. "That I would have anything to do with the death of my own wife?"

Tori swallowed at the idea that her own eyes could look just as cold to others. "It was Wraiths that brought our home down on us," Tori replied, determined to not be brought down by how much he looked like her. Looks was all that she shared with him.

"And it was the Whispers that originally unleashed Wraiths on the world. Not all Wraiths are under my control any more than all the Whispers are under yours. The Silence can use both Whispers and Wraiths to what it wishes to accomplish. There are no straight lines between good and evil like you have assumed."

"So just what should I think?" Tori asked, feeling as if she was at the end of a conversation that she wasn't as prepared for as she originally thought.

"You need to believe that we must work together if we are to stand a chance against the Silence that is coming for us all. Good and evil working together in the face of complete oblivion, the true Hell."

"Work together, eh? That sounds real promising considering that you left my mother to raise me entirely alone till her death. I can only guess that you dug up my sister's grave to send me searching for her and ultimately find her in the Silence.

Why should I think that this little charity effort on your part is nothing more than to get what you want from us and then be easily rid of us?" Tori asked, not swayed by his preaching.

"Those thugs who attacked Catherine were sent by the Silence's Hush, as well as the men who attacked you in the alleyway who then mysteriously died without you laying a hand on them. The one who we are up against has no regard for the lives it uses and takes. The government has pulled away its support from us not only because of the Arc incident, but because it doesn't believe that we stand a chance of winning. Particularly as the 'God in the Machine' has proven ineffective in protecting us."

"You mean that machine that Kali had been hooked up to?" Tori asked with concern.

"Kali had been close, but ultimately she was not strong enough to unleash its complete potential. She had been able to use it to control Wraiths, but not the Whispers. The Silence's Hush can control Wraiths and Whispers, and as you have seen firsthand, even the Hush so deeply connected to them."

"So you're saying that you tried to replicate this Machine?"

"We built a stronger one." Philip looked back outside the window. "All of Hades is sustained by the Machine. We use the energy emitted by the Wraiths to power everything. We do not need electricity from the city's grid. If the Silence's Hush were to get control of Hades, there would be nothing that can stop her. Hence, my home has become my most dangerous enemy."

"Oh, just great," Tori grumbled. "And

what about the gargoyles? Kali still have hers?"

"Yes, but if the Silence gets control of them, then it won't just be the Machine that destroys us."

"We have to send them all back. That's the only way to stop the Silence."

"What makes you say this?" Philip asked.

"Because that's what Yvon said, and it's also the only theory I have at the moment."

"If we stand together, we have a chance," Philip assured her.

"Did you set the fire at the Institute?"

"No, that was a mob of angry citizens. The public has been increasing its attacks against our kind."

"And where is my sister's body?"

"I had her buried here, with your mother. While it stands, this is the safest place in the world right now, and I wanted them here with me."

"In Hades, how wonderful," Tori added bitterly and then took notice to the dark lines on the palms of his hands. She remembered how Matthew claimed to have seen the same thing on Jade's hands. "Why are they black?" Tori asked and pointed at his hands, determined to get as much information from him as she could.

Philip looked at his palms. "It takes life force energy to walk in the Walkway. The only way to restore this lost life energy is to take it."

"Take it from who? Or should I guess?"

"People die all the time. It's simply a matter of being in the right place at the right time."

Tori didn't like how he had answered her at all.

"We cannot find the Silence's Hush individually. Both of us have tried and so far failed. If we are to stop this threat before it is too late, we must work together," Philip said and started walking towards the door. "I will let you talk about this with your friends. You are free to look around as you please while you come to your decision."

Tori watched as Cae and Matthew came back into the room when her father left, then looked back out the window. This wasn't Hell that she was in--it was limbo between those who cared about human life and those who took it like it was theirs to take all along.

Matthew walked closer to her. "Whatever you choose, we're behind you a hundred percent."

"He already told you?" Tori asked.

"Yeah..." Cae answered.

Tori let out a long sigh as the choice of leaving and roughing it out in the streets wasn't an option, either. She couldn't let her hate for Kali interfere with her responsibility to protect everyone. One way or another, it was going to be an interesting reunion. Hopefully one that didn't start and end with them trying to kill each other. If what Yvon said was true, then the only way she was going to be able to win was if she washed the regret out of her mind, once and for all.

24

TORI OPENED HER eyes to find herself lying down on the bed in her loaned room. She sat up and let out a long yawn, then looked around the dark room. She looked at the dresser and the analog clock on it that read 4:50am. Not feeling tired anymore, she got to her feet and decided to look around Hades as the place seemed to be quieter at night.

Tori left her room and started down

the hall, and stopped before completely passing by Jade's room. She could hear an argument inside, and her curiosity brought her to lean against the wall next to the slightly ajar door.

"This has gone too far! I should never have let you do it!"

"It's either us or them. I'm not going to just stand aside and let us die!" Kenji shouted back at Jade.

"This isn't right--if Tori finds out, then we are as good as dead! We can't survive out there alone."

"Tori, Tori, Tori. It's always her! Did you ever stop and think about yourself? About your real family right in front of you?"

Tori dared to peek into the room and could see now that Matthew had been telling the truth. Thin, black life lines ran across Jade's hands, the life force taken from other people. They were the unmistakable mark that the Japanese woman was a Wraith handler now.

To the far wall, Tori could see Jade's dragon in the moving wall as it allowed its form to slightly push the impression of itself forward. She concluded that Wraiths and Whispers were more alike than she could have imagined. It depended on their handler.

It wasn't that she was not prepared for the possibility of it, but it was that no matter how much she tried to accept it, the more it hurt. It also explained how Jade and her family might have survived the attack on her Institute where the others, along with everyone in them, had been completely destroyed. They could have cheated death by retreating into the safety of the Walkway.

"I'm so sorry," Jade cried.

Tori snapped out of her reverie to see them both standing in front of her now. She wanted to think that Jade had done this because she had run out of life force while protecting the Four Winds Institute, and Tori had only herself to blame for that. Exactly when and where the woman had given up to the darkness wasn't a question she was ever going to ask.

"Please don't blame this on Jade," Kenji pleaded. "I was the one who forced it on her. If anyone should be--"

"Just stop it," Tori replied angrily. "It doesn't matter anymore. We're allies with the Diruo until we find this Silence's Hush and take her out."

"And after that?" Jade asked, wiping a tear from her eye. She was trembling now.

Tori wasn't sure if Jade actually thought she would try and hurt her. "After that you're free to do whatever you want.

It's not like we were ever a real family or anything."

"Please don't say that," Jade pleaded and caught Tori's hands. "You are my family. All of what has happened can't destroy that."

"Family..." Tori paused in thought for a moment as she thought about her own. Her mother was dead because of Wraiths, her father was the leader of the Diruo. The only family she had left now was Cae and Matthew. If something happened to them because of her... "You're right, I have things to do. I'm sure that Kali can help you with...with this," Tori said in reference to Jade's hands.

"The life lines taken from--"

"The lives of others, I know," Tori interrupted Jade. It was taking all of her strength to not completely lose it on her.

"It's more than that, Tori. Just let my

aunt explain," Kenji asked.

"I've already heard the crash course of how it works. I get your reasons for doing this, I really do. If I'm mad at anyone, it's because I wasn't strong enough to keep you from having to resort to becoming a Wraith handler."

"And when you return to the Institute? What will become of us then?" Kenji asked as his own anger was beginning to break through the expression on his face.

"This is where Wraith handlers belong. Keeping Whispers and Wraiths together for an extended period of time is not something I'm open minded to do. It just doesn't work," Tori replied as she continued down the hall.

Tori found Cae that morning in what looked like a boiler room. He was sitting alone in the hot mess of a basement in front of one of the giant water tanks, seemingly deep in thought as he didn't seem to notice her approach. Facing the wet floor with his eyes closed, she wondered if he was using his unique ability to control a Whisper somewhere. It was more likely that he was trying to find any that would venture into the Wraith base at all. "Cae?"

"Oh, hey," he said and looked up at her as if she had woken him while he was dreaming awake.

"I think this is the first time I've ever seen you look more stressed out than me," Tori said and sat down next to him.

"I just haven't been able to sleep much."

"I can't blame you. This whole place is one giant nightmare, officially."

"It's just for now. The repairs to the school will be done soon and we'll be out of here," Cae said reassuringly and set his hand on her leg, putting some of her worries at ease. "Did you have a talk with Kali yet?"

"Ugh," was all that Tori could reply to that.

"Guess not. Just don't let her convert you to the dark side. I've had your father trying to do just that with me."

"Seriously? That heartless prick," Tori said, uncaring to what Wraith might be eavesdropping on them.

"Eh, for an evil warlord he's not that bad. I see where you get your talents as one, though."

"Very funny," Tori replied with a smile, as she knew he was just trying to cheer her up, despite being as weighed down with problems as she was. "So what Whisper were you in just now?"

"Well, that's the thing. I've been trying

to get into Pug lately, cause I was curious to where you were at, and I still can't."

"Pug is gone," Tori replied flatly.

"He isn't completely gone. There's something of the original Pug in there somewhere. What concerns me is that whatever is controlling him right now is blocking me out..."

"Is that what you think?"

"Pug lost his original voice, whether it was one soul or a collection of them."

"You're saying that someone is using him to spy on us?"

"The fire at the Institute and everything leading up to being here has been too organized. You need to talk to Kali and see if she's a spy for starters."

"No, I don't think it is her doing it."

"What makes you say that?" Cae asked.

"When Pug was Pug, he spoke to me

and apologized--almost as if he was family. Kali doesn't have it in her to talk like that, certainly not to me."

"Did Yvon say anything about Pug?"

"I don't think it was her, either. You can't really do much of anything in the Silence." Tori looked at him with an expression of concern. "That Hush who attacked me is going to come here. I wouldn't be surprised if we left open the door for her."

"So we need a defense plan then."

"No, we need an evacuation one. If this Hush is powerful enough to control me, she likely can do the same with Kali. I see no other reason why that Wraith Hush would have run back to my father, otherwise. If she can control us, she can bring this whole place down on us if she wants."

"If you do team up with Kali, by some

haphazard miracle, will both of you be able to stop her?"

"It's an idea. And I hate it," Tori said and started out of the boiler room to find her Nemesis.

25

TORI COULDN'T SLEEP that night as she contemplated how to approach Kali, if she did manage to find the woman in this place at some point. She had wasted the whole day trying to do just that. Nor could she stomach sleeping underground within strangling reach of her enemies. It felt as if everything she had fought for up to now was utterly for nothing. Being amongst murderers while trying to save everyone's life at the same time wasn't working for her.

If she didn't stop the Silence, every human being on the planet would die. The words of the last Hush, Melissa, haunted her memories still. The only words she would hear from this woman before she died said that the Whispers were there to save them. If that was true, the only ones who might survive this upcoming Apocalypse were the Whisper handlers like herself, and maybe even the Wraiths, until everything returned to the dust from which it came from.

She couldn't imagine such a vast world so empty and void of people. Tori wasn't even sure she wanted to be alive to see such a thing, if only to die to the despair of her failures later on. "Some Hush I am."

"I wouldn't be so harsh on yourself.

You're not the only one blinded one by this threat."

Tori looked to her side from where she sat on the rooftop inside Hades as Kali appeared from the Walkway. The only thing that kept her from lashing out at the young woman was the fact that she was walking, and not a cripple in the least. "You look improved since I saw you last."

"I didn't think you would so much as notice," Kali said as she looked down at her own two legs.

"Did you swallow a lizard and grow them back?"

"No, actually. One of the useful things of becoming a Wraith handler is that your body is easily manipulated with the Silence's dark energy. I regained my arms and legs this way. Then I realized its true purpose and separated myself from it just in time. Fortunately, my brother seems to have a certain talent with just that as we have both seen now."

Tori thought on what Kali said for a moment. If one could regrow their limbs from the Silence, just what other impossible, immortal abilities did it give? She thought about how her sister's soul was left alone to suffer in death, all because it was trapped within the Silence.

"I'm surprised that the Silence's Hush lure wasn't strong enough to compel you to stay. What was it like to leave your sister behind in death like that?"

"What was it like to turn your back on immortality?" Tori countered.

"Immortality is clearly overrated and also the only thing we seem to agree on."

"Can't see what you would want to come back to," Tori added bitterly.

"I do love my brother, despite how much you wish otherwise. What happened when we were children was an unavoidable accident, and also our fate. Everything or almost everything happens for a reason because someone sees the need for it to happen in the future. I came back for him."

"Touching," Tori replied.

"Call it what you want. The question is why do you continue to fight? For your precious Cae?"

"That and I just couldn't die leaving the living world to you."

Kali laughed and shook her head. "I'm nothing compared to the power this Silence Hush has. I see no gain in wiping out all life on Earth. If we agree to not kill each other till we kill her, we can likely defeat her. She likely can't control two Hush at the same time, likely for the fact that it requires a great deal of concentration to simply take one. It would be to our advantage however to know who is coming after us."

"I can't remember clearly. It's as if she wiped out memory of her when she possessed me for that short time."

"Then let me see if I can see her," Kali said and reached out a hand to Tori's face.

Tori leaned back in disgust. "What are you doing?"

"Going through your memories--"

"Like hell you are."

"You are really proving to be useless. Fine, I'll just do it when you're asleep again," Kali said with a shrug.

A shiver went through Tori's body of this woman touching her at all, at any point, especially when she wasn't awake.

"As much as you like to credit yourself for the reason this Silence Hush is coming for us, she is also going to come for the Machine."

"So why can't we just shut it off?" Tori asked, already having an idea what the Wraith Hush's answer would be.

"Not until we stop the Silence's Hush. The last thing we need to do is grow her strength with even more Wraiths. Philip has gone through great lengths to build-- and fortify this place. There is even a self-destruct like what the Arc had from what I've heard. If I was this Hush, bent on annihilating us, she would come in here, possess your father, and hit the kaboom switch."

"But she won't do that, at least as long as I am here."

"You have a special secret I don't know about?" Kali asked with a raised eyebrow.

"She wants me--and likely you as well--alive. Maybe it has something to do with our control over the Whispers and Wraiths, I don't know, but she won't bring the place down with us inside. That's likely why my father is so overly concerned with keeping us comfortable here."

"I hope it's as simple as you say, otherwise this won't be the only Hell we're stuck with each other in."

"If we're stuck here, then there is another problem too," Tori added.

"Oh?" Kali asked.

"Yvon said that we can't drive the Silence back without getting all the gargoyles to return. If we're stuck in here, that means we can't go hunting for them."

"Before your sister made contact with the gargoyles, she had spoken with many of the Whispers. Millions of them started to leave on a single idea that a human girl could hold the power to not only sway them, but speak with them. It was those original Whispers that became gargoyles.

The bridge between the living and the dead was made with a simple idea that the Silence could be something other than just that--silent. Maybe even alive as a force of its own. But as you know now, that bridge is also what will bring destruction to humankind. The dead and living were never meant to be on the same plane of existence."

"So you're saying that all this was my sister's fault? How can you blame this Apocalypse on one little girl!?"

"Civilizations have fallen to much less," Kali said.

"I can't believe what you're saying," Tori replied. She pressed her fingers to her forehead, trying to force the idea of her own sister being responsible for all this out of her head.

"I really don't care if you believe me or not, it makes no difference as what has happened as a result of your sister is already clearly evident. Yet I have an idea on how to get the gargoyles to go back, but we need your sister to show us where they all are."

"Back into the Silence for me, great," Tori said aloud.

"Once we know where they are, I'm going to need your boyfriend to get them all back," Kali said with a wry grin. "He likely doesn't realize it himself, but he's one of the few Tueri skilled enough to possess and move a gargoyle next to us."

"The Silence isn't somewhere you can just walk a gargoyle back into."

"It is if the love of your life is there," Kali added and then turned to leave. "There is only one way we're going to win this war, and that is if we swear to ourselves to never look back. If we look back, we will lose this fight and we will lose everything of this world with it. I'm starting to think that we were chosen for our lack of regrets."

"Never look back?" Tori pondered on just how hard that could be. She was nothing more than a walking regret, constantly looking back at all the places where she tripped up.

"Sodom and Gomorrah," Vincent's voice said from the direction of the door to the roof.

"Isn't that the story in the Bible where people turn to salt because they looked back at their city being destroyed?" Tori asked Vincent. She wondered if his stalking had anything to do with how Cae was seemingly avoiding of her as of late.

"Yes, it was Lot's wife. His family was warned to flee the city of sins and not look back, but she did."

"Now that you brought this

conversation up," Tori replied, "Is there some great Biblical story behind gargoyles?"

"Some ask forgiveness for their sins and pass into the afterlife," Kali added. "Some linger here, often as Wraiths and angry spirits. Or as Whispers who feel they have to finish something they were unable to when alive. Gargoyles refuse to accept any kind of final judgment altogether, and they become a combination of many voices set on serving the living world, or escalating its destruction."

Vincent walked over to Tori's side to take in the view with her. "And your eyes will be open, and you will be as gods, having knowledge of good and evil."

"Yeah, some gods we're turning out to be. So what do you really want?" she snapped at him. All he had to do was be near her and she would become angry and she didn't know if it was their past or his cockiness that triggered it.

"Easy, I'm not here to fight," he said and lifted his hands in surrender. "Have you decided what you're going to do?" Vincent asked.

"We can't just sit around and accept this dark judgment, nor can we dwell in the past. It won't stop at what happened to my mother. This whole thing is just stupid and it's the reason why this Silence's Hush is having a field day with us--she doesn't have a rulebook to follow. What's the point of working with the bad guys if you can't make some valid use of them?" Tori thought aloud.

"Diruo Evil Headquarters, at your service," Vincent said with a mock bow.

"Cae's mom thinks that it's someone who knows me--who I clearly pissed off at some point in my life," Tori said.

"Just how many potentials are we dealing with?" Vincent asked with concern.

"A lot," Tori replied. "But I can handle whoever it turns out to be, as long as I don't look back. It's a weak plan at best."

A smile went across Vincent's face. "Does this new rule of yours apply to me too?"

"No," Tori replied in an emotionless tone.

Vincent let out a long sigh at that and shrugged his shoulders as he followed his sister out of the room to help with the preparations.

26

TORI WAS STARTING to regret taking a tour of Hades that night, only starting with how she couldn't find Matthew anywhere. She found what was likely Kali's Hush chamber by instinct alone. All of the negative energy of the underground facility felt as if it flowed here. Then there was the not-so-common sight of a hundred faces moving within the door to it. All of it felt like a really bad horror movie.

"Aren't you a cheerful one?"

"I wish you Diruo would stop doing that," Tori said as she kept her eyes on the terrifying wall as Vincent appeared out of nowhere behind her.

"Awe, we're not THAT spooky."

"This has to be the worst set of circumstances I have ever been stuck in," Tori replied.

"It's not that bad. Look, the Wraiths haven't even screamed at you. If I didn't know better, I'd say you were rather intimidating," Vincent said with a mocking tone.

"Very funny. Your sense of humor is as sad as your attempt to be my friend."

"Your father does offer a rather hefty reward for every effort of winning your trust, just so you can't say I didn't tell you the truth of my intentions. So here is my latest offering for a fraction of your trust, and not too late after your birthday," Vincent said and handed Tori a picture of a young woman with long, dark hair.

"Who is this?" Tori asked, recognizing the face but with uncertainty.

"My sister and I have been snooping around in your nightmares for the last week trying to figure that out, and we kept seeing her. See, when a Hush messes with someone alive, it leaves a trace of them in the form of memories on the person they messed with. But all we have been able to put together so far is that this person is someone from your past, and they're attached to a lot of your regret. Do you recognize her?"

"I don't know."

"You don't know or you don't want to remember?" Vincent asked.

"Both. I don't want to paint a target on

someone for you to kill."

"If we can capture her alive, then we will. We need you to stop worrying about this woman and have all your strength and focus in order to find your sister in the Silence again."

Tori didn't say anything. If it was someone from her past, she didn't want to set a hit squad of Diruo after them.

"Tori, if we can stop her, we can stop this Silence."

"She's only a small piece of it," Tori replied. "Killing her will just give rise to another in her place. We have to stick to the get the gargoyles back plan."

"Okay, well it may give rise to a new Silence Hush, but they likely won't be interested in specifically killing you."

"Just forget it," Tori said. "I don't want to talk about anyone else dying."

"Fine," Vincent said and put the

picture back into his pocket. "But you're not going into the Silence alone. If anything, I'm going to have to beg Yvon for forgiveness in the hope we can get her to cooperate with us."

"Do what you want. Just don't kill anyone in the meantime, okay?" Tori said.

"Alright," Vincent said and turned to leave. "And Matthew is right there," he added randomly and pointed at the door.

Tori followed Vincent out of Kali's Hush chamber and looked down to where Matthew was sitting next to the door, busily typing into his laptop. "There you are."

"I must be doing a good job of stalking you if you only found me now..." Matthew said and closed his laptop before looking up at her. They looked to see Cae join up with them. "So what's the plan?"

"I have to go back into the Silence for

some directions on where to find all of these gargoyles. Vincent will be in charge of getting me out. Cae, you need to follow Kali as I tell her where the gargoyles are, and then take them over and bring them here. It will be a message that likely has to relay off of a few Whispers and Wraiths to reach you, and I hope their ears are good in the Walkway. Jade, Kenji and you, Matthew, need to hold off the Silence's Hush should she decide to drop in while we're doing all this. Once we have the gargoyles back in the Silence, the Wraiths and Whispers will theoretically follow. The only thing that can mess this plan up is the Silence Hush unleashing the furious Wraiths from within the Machine on us before we get the not-so-angry ones under control."

"There is one thing you're leaving out," Matthew said. "What if the gargoyles don't want to go back?"

"If Yvon really did unleash them, then they will return if she tells them to come back, along with some motivation from Kali and me," Tori answered. "Worst case scenario, I will use Pug for more positive reinforcement and drag them back," Tori said.

"Then they might put up a fight, too," Cae added.

"Then we fight back," Tori said and looked at Vincent. "The only gargoyle I'm particularly worried about is the massive one I saw in the Silence. I get the feeling he doesn't answer to anyone."

"Just how big was it?" Cae asked curiously.

"About half the height of my old building, and I couldn't see around it."

"Oh joy," Cae replied. "Let's deal with that one last if we have to."

"Agreed," Tori said.

27

TORI HAD AN impossible time trying to get Pug to come to her, or at the very least, make some kind of indication that he could hear her at all. Frustrated, she used the other Whispers to track him down in Hades to what looked like an executive office. To her surprise, she found her father standing next to Pug. She had been going out of her way to avoid the man, only to run into him now when she least wanted to. She cursed herself for not anticipating this trap.

"You will forgive me for being rather distant lately. The Walkway's cost is great on one's life energy and Hades as itself can be rather time consuming."

"I wasn't looking for you," Tori replied angrily and contemplated just leaving faster than she had come into the room.

"Do give me a few minutes. I know that it is impossible for me to make up for the countless years that we have lost between us."

Tori was tapping her foot now as if her impatience might make his sentiment go faster. It felt like it was taking forever. "What do you want?"

"I don't have much time left, but I will try to explain the reason for my actions as best I can."

"Don't Wraith handlers use the energy

of the dead to stay going forever?"

"That is true," Philip replied. "But I'm not like the other Wraith handlers. It comes as a cost for the destiny I have chosen for myself. Before my time is up, however, I need you to understand that I did everything in my power to save your mother."

"Oh, right," Tori replied, growing increasingly angry. "In the comfort of your evil headquarters, no doubt you were going to get right on it after you've completed taking over the world."

"No, Tori. I was there when it happened."

Tori forced her mind back to the painful memory when her entire apartment building came crashing down. She thought of the men she had seen outside before it happened. She thought about every face she saw before the building crushed her mother and spared her on account of Pug pulling her into the Walkway. She felt her thoughts stop on Pug.

"It was impossible to pull her into the Walkway, as unlike myself and Deron, she never had a direct affinity with its death energy. There was nothing I could do to save her, but I believe that in stopping the Silence, we can prevent such a disaster from happening again."

"You are the reason the Silence is out of control as it is! Your Hades Machine has enraged the Wraiths to what they are now."

"They had already become uncontrollable. Hades was meant to be a band-aid to the amount of damage they can cause, not a permanent solution. You hate me, and I understand. Until you are a parent yourself, you will not understand any of my actions. Using the Silence to empower us, it makes you into a target for all your enemies, past, and future. It is their hate that drives them and I did not want you anywhere near that, and sadly that meant keeping my distance from you. But the age-old saying of how one cannot defeat hate with hate is very true. That is the real reason I need you to set things right. You love your friends and you want this world to survive. I believe that love is strong enough to set things back to normal in this world again."

"It's really cute how everyone expects me to save the world, but I'm starting to think it's a bit much."

"It was your sister who had a significant part in bringing the Whispers and Wraiths into our world, and I believe that you can send them back to their own plane of existence. I believe this because you are my daughter."

Tori had heard about all she could bear and looked at Pug to command him to come to her, but he didn't move from the stone that he had been sitting in. "Are you why Pug isn't as he was before?"

Philip smiled and laid a hand on the base of one of Pug's wings. The gargoyle came back to life and looked at Tori with its yellow eyes.

She had been so transfixed for that moment that Philip had vanished from standing beside him in the same instant. *Damn Diruo*, she thought to herself and walked over to Pug. "So were you thinking of responding at any point?" she grumbled at him. Without warning, he lifted an arm and pulled her into a hug just like he had so long ago on her balcony when she had first demanded answers from him. It was the Pug she had lost, returned. But something about her father having vanished moments before made it all feel so eerily uncomfortable. She started to head out of the office and Pug followed on all fours, so she decided to worry about thinking more about it later. Right now, she had to get back into the Silence and get to work at helping to save the world.

28

EVERYONE SEEMED ON edge when Tori returned to Kali's Hush chamber with Pug. She knew that they had every right to be, but something about this time seemed different.

"There you are," Cae said and went over to her. "You haven't by chance seen your father?"

"I was just talking to him in what I think was his office. Why, what's going on?" Tori asked in concern.

"The alarms just went off that his tracking signal hasn't returned for some minutes now. If what Vincent says about him not being a Wraith handler is true, he can't just up and vanish."

Tori suddenly felt very cold as she looked back to where Pug was sitting calmly and listening to their conversation. "What do you mean he's not a Wraith handler? Then what the hell is he?" She was answered by the ground suddenly shaking around them, and what sounded like all of Hades coming to a grinding halt.

"Please tell me you didn't kill him..." Cae pleaded.

"I didn't do anything to him. He just like vanished before my eyes, and now you're telling me that he can't do something like that?" Tori was now officially freaking out.

"Well someone is attempting to lock down Hades," Vincent said as he walked closer to them and confirmed just that with his sister as she emerged from the Walkway. "And it's not your father."

Tori pressed her knuckles to her forehead, then looked at Pug. The gargoyle had turned to stone, and she wondered if it had anything to do with her father's disappearance. She closed her eyes and reopened them into the Walkway, and Pug looked at her with his yellow eyes when she did. "What's going on?"

"The Silence's Hush is near. I'm locking down Hades, but I don't know how long it will be possible to keep her out. You have to get working on your plan, now."

Tori shook her head as his familiar voice sent a chill down her spine. But the idea that her father was Pug was crazy, and she was already overflowing with nuts as it were. She left the Walkway and looked then at Vincent. "Pug says we have to initiate our plan like right now." When there was no argument to it, she looked then at Cae. "Will you still be able to get in and out of Hades with it locked down like this?"

"He'll have help," Kali said. "The Wraiths are still responding to me."

Tori looked at Vincent again. "We'll have to find Philip later. You ready to go?"

"Whenever you are," Vincent said.

"If it gets dangerous in there, you immediately bring her back," Cae warned Vincent.

"Just don't let my sister do anything reckless in the meantime and this will work," Vincent replied, then turned and vanished into the Walkway.

Cae went over to Tori and hugged her, then kissed her hair. "Be careful and come back."

Tori held onto him tight. "I will. I'll be more worried about you and your work partner," Tori replied and reluctantly let go of him.

"Focus on finding out where all the gargoyles are and don't worry about me. Crazy women have become my specialty thanks to you," Cae teased.

Tori just shook her head and then took in a deep breath, before nodding and following Vincent into the Walkway. On opening her eyes to a darkened world, she set her thoughts on finding Yvon, and could feel her heart begin to pull her towards her sister. Pug picked her up in one hand, and Vincent in his other, as if they were nothing more than large dolls to the gargoyle. Then the gargoyle spread its wings in the direction that Tori looked.

29

IT DIDN'T TAKE long to find Yvon as Pug landed them in the center of the city as it was in the Walkway and set them down. Her sister didn't look at them when they approached, only remained on her knees, staring at the ground. "Sister, are you alright?" It was the dumbest question she could possibly ask, as having one's soul forever stuck in the Silence was anything, but 'alright.'

"She will be fine, once you surrender, Tori," another voice said from the shadows made by the Silence's dark energy around them.

"Is that the Hush?" Vincent asked and looked around for her as he stood ready for anything.

"Yeah," Tori said as she looked in the direction that Pug did, which likely was exactly where the Hush was. Vincent caught on fast enough, and his chimera started to close in on the building from one side, while they made their way closer via the other. "What have you done with my sister?"

"Well, you already know the rules, Tori. There can only be one Hush in charge. Your sister was quite the accomplished Hush, and seeing as I intend to command the entire world of Whispers and Wraiths, there is also no room for her to continue to exist."

Vincent grabbed Tori before she could run further ahead of him to tear the Silence's Hush apart.

"So you will understand that we can no longer be friends, as I must eradicate you from all existences," the Hush continued.

Tori looked up as the darkness of the Walkway suddenly became a whole lot darker, and Vincent, who had been holding her a moment before, had vanished. "So this is what you did to my sister? Lock her in a deeper darkness than the Walkway can already offer?" There was no answer, and Tori took in a deep breath to calm herself. Fear and her hatred of this Hush would get her trapped in here forever. She had to see the light where there was none.

She closed her eyes and reopened them, and saw a flicker of a soul's light in the distance. Tori sped off towards it and found her sister and her consciousness looking back at her.

"That woman is going to destroy everything. You have to stop her," Yvon pleaded.

"I know, I intend to. I'm going to bring all the gargoyles back, but you have to help me find them."

"There isn't enough time--"

"I have help. I just need yours now."

Yvon stood up and touched Tori's forehead. "You have to make the good ones see that being in our world causes more harm than good. If you can rally them on this, then they will help you return all the Wraiths as well. Without them, the Silence's Hush will be powerless."

"That's the plan." Tori looked closer as Yvon vanished for a moment, before the scene of where the first gargoyle was in the city flashed before her eyes. She didn't fight the visions, and let them come to her, jotting them to a memory they were already being set into. When it was over, she looked at her sister who started to cry.

"You have to forget about me now. You have to focus on the ones you love who are still alive, and you have to be true to yourself. Good luck, sister, and goodbye."

Yvon vanished before Tori could say anything in turn, and she looked at Vincent, who looked to be having nothing short of a panic attack from the absence of her consciousness.

"Tori!"

"I know where they are. Buy me some time and I'll help you pummel this witch into the ground."

That was all he needed to hear to know she was back, and he looked to his chimera as it launched itself against the woman who was now standing where Yvon had been a moment before.

Tori ran to Pug and grabbed the gargoyle's snout, before sending all of her thoughts into him like a barrage of memories. The gargoyle froze up for a moment, but it then closed its yellow eyes and sent all of it to the Whispers that were near Cae and Kali.

With the message sent, she focused on helping Vincent as a rush of the Silence's energy crashed into him from the side and hurled him across the dark ground. She charged at the woman, before stopping with her fist intended for the Hush's face. "Mary?"

Mary smiled a malevolent smile at her, before striking her down with the back of her hand.

Tori was dazed and confused for a

moment after her behind collided with the ground, and she quickly tried to recover. "Why are you doing this?"

"You know why I'm doing this. This world doesn't need any more pain or suffering the likes of what I had to endure."

"You know her?" Vincent asked, wiping a streak of blood away from the side of his mouth with his hand.

"Yeah, and this old friendship is going to die hard." Tori got to her feet and brought her full focus on ending the young woman she helped create.

"But we can be friends again. All you have to do is prove your undying devotion to me by ending his life," Mary said and looked at Vincent.

"There's just one problem with your request."

"And what's that?" Mary asked.

"I care about him more than the murderer you've become."

"Really?" Vincent asked optimistically.

"Yeah, but I'm still going to kick your ass next."

Vincent's chimera pounced on Mary from behind, and Vincent followed its attack with his own, and landed a punch across the Silence's Hush face.

The woman growled at him, and lifted her hand and struck him back with another wave of dark energy. "Then you will both die, just as your sister and lover are already dead."

A chill went down Tori's spine at the thought of something having happened to Cae, but Vincent quickly called her attention back to the present.

"They're both fine. I can hear my sister's voice and they almost have all the gargoyles."

Tori nodded with a renewed reassurance and looked at Pug then. The gargoyle grabbed Mary in its claws, and the young woman struggled in futility to break free of the monster's grasp. "Your powers won't work on this one."

"Damn you! I will not stop until you're dead!" Mary hissed at her.

Then without any command, Pug snapped the neck of the woman with his powerful claws and set her back on the floor.

A state of disbelief went through Tori all at once as a frozen chill.

"Tori?"

"I didn't..." Tori said in her defense.

"No, you didn't," Pug added. "I refuse to lose another daughter to darkness. Now the Silence is mine to control, and I will bring it back to where it belongs. Hades is yours now, daughter."

Tori couldn't speak as Pug spread his powerful leathery wings then, and took to the air of the Walkway. It was starting to collapse like black glass all around them, before leaving them standing in the real world of their city. Only a few streets away stood the massive gargoyle that Tori and Vincent had seen before in the Walkway, once again stone.

"If that had dragged on any longer, we would be toast," Vincent said.

Tori found that she still couldn't speak as the sight of her friend dying before her eyes flashed over and over again.

"It had to be done," Vincent said in a weak attempt to try and console her.

"It could have been done differently," Tori replied as several tears escaped her eyes. She brought her focus then to trying to find Cae as the city around them looked like a war had just torpedoed through it.

30

TORI SAW CAE coming towards them and she sprinted to him and he caught her in a tight embrace. "What happened to Kali?" she asked in mild concern and looked around for her.

Cae didn't answer, only nodded in the direction of his brother, who had fallen to one knee.

"Vincent!" Tori called to him and ran back. The dark energy of the Silence that had sustained him beyond his human lifespan was returning to where it came from, erasing his body as it did so.

"It's alright. I knew the price of merging with the darkness when I did. And we saved the world, so it's not so bad."

Tori tried to grab and hold him together, but it was proving impossible.

"So, how much of forever do I have left?" Vincent asked, looking away from his fading state to hold onto her eyes.

"You can't die--not like this!" Tori cried. "Why did you help me? I never wanted anyone to die for it!"

"I know, that's why you couldn't know," Vincent said and set his dissipating hand on her cheek. "I promised you that I would make you fall in love with me, and I did, so I leave on a win. You're just going to have to kick my butt in the next life. Now stay the good kind of crazy woman that you are, cause if there's a way, you can be damn sure I'll be watching."

Tori went to grab his hand, but at that moment he exploded into ashes, leaving nothing but his clothes behind. She picked them up and held onto them tightly, fearing she would never get her tears to stop.

Cae knelt down on one knee beside her and took her hand into his. "It happened so fast with Kali, that I didn't even have a moment to process what was going on."

"Has this happened to all the Wraith handlers?" Tori asked aloud, fearing the fate of Jade and Kenji, who they had left back in Hades.

"They wouldn't want us to look back," Cae said and pulled her to her feet. We have to move forward now."

Tori wiped some of the tears off of her face and looked around them. There was no way to guess how many likely died because she had sent the Silence back. Their sacrifice was for the greater good, to save all of humanity, but she still felt like a murderer.

"It wasn't your fault. They knew the price that came with using the Silence."

"Or so I'm left to try and convince myself for the rest of my life. Vincent didn't deserve this. None of our friends deserved this."

"Tori," Cae said and tried to touch her, but she pulled away from him.

"No," Tori said and walked away from him. "I never wanted this to happen. The irony is that all this time I feared the choice you would make if given--that you would choose me and your friends and family over saving the world, and then I go and do this. I can never forgive myself for that!"

"I know. But you have to, or else their sacrifice would have been for nothing."

Tori turned away from Cae and headed in the direction of Hades, to see if there was anything left of her father's legacy.

EPILOGUE

MUCH OF HADES had collapsed in on itself, as the Silence's energy that was now gone had brought the machines to a grinding halt. Several walls had crumbled as the Wraiths that likely had made them their own were no longer inside and supporting them. The entire place now looked and felt like a dark, ancient tomb.

What was even scarier than their surroundings was the lack of noise or people around. Tori remembered how Vincent had evaporated between her very hands, and she held out her palm as ashes fell from above. She wondered how many people's lives she was responsible for snuffing out.

A light that was different from the emergency lights caught her eye, and she made her way over the ruins towards it. A wall had collapsed here, and behind it the glow proved to be coming from a green, living grotto that wasn't much different than the one back at the Institute. She stopped before two headstones; one marked with her mother's name and the other her sister's.

"It seems he buried your family in the safest place in here," Cae said as he stood next to her.

"Yeah," Tori replied and crouched before it. "Though there is likely no chance of finding Jade's or Kenji's remains." She stood up quick on remembering Matthew. She tapped her pockets, now desperately looking for the cell phone he had given her. Just as she caught it in her hand, it vibrated and started to ring. She pushed the button to answer. "Hello?"

Static noise replied.

A sense of panic began to overwhelm her now as she looked around, and then ran out of the grotto. "Matthew!"

"Hehe," he giggled and held up his own phone as he came out from behind a large piece of the broken wall. "Now we're even with the whole scaring the life out of each other thing."

Tori let out a long breath of relief, before rushing at him. He ducked, fearing she would pummel him, but instead gave him a hug.

He smiled and returned it, before pulling away. "I'm gonna go ahead and guess that you already know what happened to the Wraith handlers..."

"Yeah," Tori replied solemnly. "How many are no longer alive?"

"It's hard to say for sure as I'll have to restore the power to the computer before I can start to count the lives and extent of damage. So far, all of the Tueri seem to be okay."

"Well, we should go back to the school for now," Cae said and led the way out of the ruins.

Tori followed him, but stopped to look at a gargoyle that resembled Pug. She ran towards him and quickly looked it over, trying to figure out if it was alive. She couldn't hear it and it didn't move. She closed her eyes, trying to see its form in the Walkway, but that ability was also gone. She stepped back and took in more details of the gargoyle and realized that it looked exactly like the one at the graveyard with her nightmarish encounter with the Wraith angel. The demon had almost been right--if it hadn't been for her father, they would all be dead now. The Wraith's foresight left out the power of love and humanity would live on as a result of it. She stepped closer to the gargoyle and brushed some of the ashes and debris off its gray face and then turned to follow Cae. The statue was a reminder of what Vincent had told her. She couldn't look back, not if she hoped to ever stay ahead of the immeasurable amount of death that was now her past. And she did not see when the gargoyle turned its head to watch her go.

ABOUT THE AUTHOR

S.J. Wist is a fantasy author, reviewer, and an artist on the side. Addicted to books, blogs, chocolate mint ice cream, and all things creative. She lives in Toronto, Canada.